ALMOST OVER IT

KYLIE GILMORE

Copyright
Almost Over It © 2015 by Kylie Gilmore
Excerpt from *The Opposite of Wild* © 2014 by Kylie Gilmore

First Edition: February 2015
Cover design by Rogenna Brewer
Published by: Extra Fancy Books
Originally published under the title *Stud Unleashed: Will*

ISBN-10: 1942238053
ISBN-13: 978-1-942238-05-8

For sexy orthodontists everywhere…

CHAPTER ONE

Will Levi could count on one hand the things that were going right in his life. Two things to be exact—he was a successful orthodontist with a thriving practice, and he owned his own home. The other list—the things-gone-wrong list—was too long to count. Even his golf game was off. Suffice it to say, he was sure his blood pressure was elevated, and he was well on his way to his first heart attack at the ripe age of thirty-three.

He'd nearly had a heart attack already this morning when he'd dropped his pants in the bathroom and his cat, Sweetie, had leaped on his bare leg, just barely missing a very sensitive and important part of his anatomy. His forearms still stung from the deep gashes Sweetie had given him when Will carried him out of the bathroom.

He'd adopted Sweetie (his name from the shelter) eight months ago in a misguided attempt to make his house feel less empty after Carrie dumped him for the one person he never thought would betray him. Whatever. He'd moved on. In any case, the cat was a terrible companion. Sweetie frequently pounced on him from behind—in bed, on the sofa, on the toilet. Scratches were his reward for trying to pet Sweetie, who was, in a cruel twist, a beautiful gray and white cat with extremely soft fur. What was the point of a pet you couldn't pet? But Will felt too guilty to return Sweetie. No one in their right mind would ever adopt him, and he'd end up forever in a cage or put to sleep.

"Go to hell, Sweetie!" he called on his way out the door. The cat would surely piss in his best leather dress shoes in revenge.

He made the short drive to his office on the other side of Clover Park and noted that the new Clover Park Dance Studio occupying the other half of his building appeared to be open for the first time. Someone was walking around in there. He should introduce himself on his break and make sure the new tenant understood the parking situation. He parked his silver BMW in his reserved spot in the rear parking lot, walked in the back door of the building, and headed to his office. A flash of pink caught his eye. Through the glass door of the dance studio, he saw the woman bent over in a pink leotard with pink tights, her sweet ass facing him, firm and round, just meant for a man's hands. He got hard and quickly decided to postpone their conversation. He did an about-face, heading back to the parking lot, where he gave himself a few minutes to cool down before he returned to his office, careful not to glance next door.

"Good morning, Hillary," he said to his receptionist on the way in. "How was your weekend?"

She beamed. "Great, Dr. Levi! How was yours?"

"Can't complain."

He continued on to his private office, slipped on the white coat embroidered with his name, and checked the day's schedule on his laptop. He stared at the schedule, not really seeing it. Who was that woman in pink? He'd introduce himself properly as soon as he had a chance. He checked his schedule for real this time. He had half an hour before his first appointment. Maybe he could—

"Morning, everyone!" Dr. Tony Russo, his coworker, called cheerfully.

Will ground his back teeth as Tony poked his head in Will's office, wearing a Yankees cap sideways along with shades and a half-unbuttoned shirt that showed off massive amounts of dark chest hair. A thick gold chain necklace with a giant gold molar dangled from the end, nestled in the hair. "Hey, Dr. Will!"

"Dr. Russo, what do you think you're doing?" His outfit was not approved for office wear.

Tony held up his palms and turned side to side. "You like the duds?"

"No."

"Someone needs their morning coffee." Tony grinned. "I got you a necklace too." He produced another gold molar necklace from a bag along with an identical Yankees cap. Will was a Red Sox fan until the day he died.

"You keep it," Will said as politely as possible.

Tony perched on the edge of Will's desk, sitting on some patient files. Will gestured for him to move. Tony lifted a butt cheek and handed him the files.

"Thanks," Will ground out.

"Dr. Will—"

"It's Dr. Levi."

"Dr. Levi," Tony amended with a small smile. "Most of our patients are teens, right?"

Will said nothing. He refused to answer rhetorical questions. He'd brought Tony on board two months ago to help with the increasing patient load and had been regretting the decision ever since. Tony seemed so normal at first. He'd worn a bow tie to the interview, as Will wore every day, and had been enthusiastic about correcting malocclusions. Tony had also recently graduated from a highly competitive graduate orthodontics program and, upon questioning, was knowledgeable on the latest techniques as well as proven methods.

And then Tony started work. It had been one nightmare after another as Tony put his questionable "Tony touch" on everything. He and Will had already gone five rounds on why a capuchin monkey in a glass cage wasn't appropriate for an orthodontists' office. Tony felt it would be therapeutic and a nice distraction for the patients enduring the long appointment required to apply braces. Will felt it would be insane.

Tony set the necklace and offending cap on Will's desk. Like Will would ever appear as Tweedle Dee and Tweedle Dum in front of his patients.

"We can be the rapping docs," Tony said. "Really reach the teens in their wheelhouse, know what I mean?"

Will made a herculean effort not to throw the offending gifts in the garbage. Instead, with the patience that would surely mark him as a saint, he said, "Tony, I appreciate the sentiment, but rapping is not what patients come here for. They expect a high level of care and results. That's what we give them here at Levi Orthodontics." He threw in that last bit to remind Tony that he was the junior orthodontist here and not the decision-maker.

Unfortunately, Tony started to rap.

He breathed heavily into his palm with multiple

clicks and spitting noises before barking:

> "Keeping teeth safe.
> With braces.
> No gum.
> No Starburst.
> Keeping it real, yo!
> There be prizes.
> Kickin' it."

Tony finished his rap with a large criss-crossed arm gesture and looked to Will for his response. Will's blood pressure elevated into the red zone. And then some truly awful boy-band music blasted through the room. He left rapping Tony to tell Hillary to turn the music down only to find that it wasn't from his office at all. It was coming from across the hall at the dance studio. Now they had to talk about the parking situation and acceptable noise levels for a shared building space.

He marched across the hall and was about to knock on the glass door when he caught sight of the woman inside and froze. He could see her clearly through the large windows of the waiting room. Her palms were flat on the floor as she bent at the waist, her long legs and very sweet ass facing him again. He felt himself grow warmer as he watched her go through a series of stretches. She still had her back to him, so he kept watching. Her dark brown hair was in a tight bun, her tanned skin glowed, her body moved like a dream, and he couldn't tear himself away. She shook out her arms and legs, then did a joyful twirl in the air. He found himself smiling and, without a second thought, opened the door to the studio. A chime went off announcing his arrival, and she stopped her solo dance and turned to face him. His smile dropped.

Jasmine Davis. The aggravating woman he'd fought with all summer at the Eastman community theater's production of *The Pirates of Penzance*. Last summer had been the perfect storm of things gone wrong, and Jasmine had been the cherry on top. That sounded too delicious. She'd been the straw that broke the camel's back—a long, willowy…beautiful straw. No, she was just one more *aggravation* piled on top. The woman was too aggressive, too in-your-face, and way too loosey-goosey about music that was intended to be played a certain way by the composer. Why have sheet music, why compose anything at all, if you weren't going to play it the right way?

She crossed to the waiting room and narrowed her dark brown eyes. "Are you spying on me, Will Levi?"

See, right away, confrontational.

"You," he ground out.

His dad had neglected to mention he'd rented the space to Jasmine. He'd just said he'd rented it to a wonderful young lady. Ha. Good one, Dad.

She cocked her head to the side. "Can I help you with something?" She looked behind him. "Are you lost?"

"I am not lost. I work across the hall, and I came over here to ask you to please keep the music to a low roar."

She muttered a curse under her breath, spun on her heel, and turned the volume down the tiniest bit possible. "Happy?" she called over the grating be-bop of boys with too-long hair and too much teen spirit.

He crossed to her side and turned the music down to an acceptable level. "Yes."

She turned it back up. "It's a dance studio. I need music."

He turned it back down. "I don't need to hear your choice of music all day while I'm working on patients."

She turned it back up. "They'll love it."

He turned it back down. "I'll hate it. This is called noise pollution."

She jabbed a finger in his chest. "This is called get out of my studio before I kick your ass."

His lips twitched. The idea of Jasmine kicking his ass was absurd. Sure, she was athletic, but he had four inches and at least forty pounds on her. Not only that, he lifted weights. With her slender arms, she probably couldn't lift more than a three-pound dumbbell. He kept that to himself, though, because women hated when you brought up obvious facts such as that.

"Jazzy," he said just to bug her. It was an old nickname her younger sister Zoe was allowed to call her and no one else. It was how he ended all their arguments this summer. It was damn lucky he'd overheard Zoe say it at play rehearsal. She glanced at his crotch, which he knew was bulging after he'd admired her ass (before he knew it was her). Dammit. He wished she'd stop doing that. She always seemed to notice his bulge this summer too; so freaking embarrassing the way his body responded against his will.

She did a head swivel and returned to the center of the dance floor.

She danced freely.

He watched unwillingly.

She caught him watching and gave him a knowing smile to go along with a full-body wave, her hands running down her torso, a move that flirted between dance and foreplay.

He turned and marched back to his office, blood pressure throbbing in the one place he didn't want to rise for *that woman*, and slammed the door.

CHAPTER TWO

Jasmine finished her first day of classes exhilarated by the experience. She'd been dreaming of owning her own dance studio for years. She'd needed a break from the cycle of grueling auditions, rejections, and cutthroat competition for lead dance roles on Broadway. Truthfully, the shine had worn off a year into it when she'd landed her first Broadway show at nineteen and naively gotten involved with the show's choreographer, stupidly thinking she was in love for the first time. The mistake had taught her a harsh lesson on letting people in too soon.

She locked up, exited the building, and went up the back stairs to her apartment over the studio. The rent on the apartment was a real bargain, and she knew that was due to her friendship with Brian Levi, the landlord. She'd worked for years with him at the summer community theater where he was the pianist, until last summer when his son, Will, took his place.

She let herself in and headed to the kitchen to make herself a tuna-fish sandwich for dinner. She knew Will was trouble the very first day she'd met him. At first, she'd thought he was kinda cute standing there at the piano, talking to their director, Toby. He wore black-rimmed vintage-style glasses, a red bow tie, white button-down shirt, and pressed beige trousers. The outfit screamed cool hipster and was a look she knew well from her friends in the city. She approached, eager to meet Brian's son, and waited while Toby finished his conversation with Will. She glanced down, noticed Will was hung, and quickly looked away. She wasn't a total perv. Years of working with men in tights told her at a glance what they had going on. And while size supposedly didn't matter, her personal experience told her it very much did.

Toby had introduced them.

"It's so nice to meet you," she said warmly.

Will had stared at her hair, which she'd left down in all its untamed curly glory. Then he stared at her mouth, then her neck, before he finally mumbled, "Nice to meet you."

Toby left them alone.

"I'm the choreographer," she said, "so I'm sure we'll be working closely together this summer. How's your dad?"

He finally met her eyes and spoke, and it was in

that fateful moment that she realized he was way too rigid and uptight to ever pull off cool hipster.

"My dad is fine," he said in a clipped voice. "He's drinking his way across the Atlantic on a last-minute cruise while I got roped into this job." He scowled. "Like I don't have a million other things I need to do this summer."

Jasmine deflated. Summer community theater was supposed to be fun. People joined just for the hell of it. Only she and the director got paid; everyone else volunteered. It wasn't cutthroat or competitive like Broadways shows. Will's attitude was going to put a damper on everything.

She tried again. "The music this year is so much fun. Have you gotten a chance to play it yet?"

"No, but I will play it accurately," he said. "I'm a competent pianist."

Maybe his blood sugar was low. That could make a person cranky. "Would you like a butterscotch candy?" she asked. "I have some in my purse."

He stared at her mouth. She gestured toward the front row of the auditorium where her purse sat. "Should I get one?" she asked.

"Let me tell you about the mouth's response to hard candy." And before she could say, *no, thank you, loser*, he launched into a long lecture about how, if a person absolutely had to eat candy, a candy bar would be preferable because sucking on hard candy made the sugar coat the teeth and some more mumbo jumbo about saliva and chemistry and tooth enamel.

She held up a hand. "Forget it."

He smirked, and her hackles rose. She turned on her heel and walked away before she ended up yelling at him to loosen the hell up.

As rehearsals wore on, he drove her absolutely bat-shit crazy. He refused to slow the music so she could get the police brigade—a group of extremely uncoordinated men—to follow the basic dance steps without tripping over each other. He also refused to stop and correct those that were out of tune. Just let them keep on going, messing everything up. His dad had always worked *with* her. Will seemed to make it his mission to aggravate her more.

And the way he called her Jazzy. Ugh! Zoe called her that because she couldn't say the "s" in Jasmine when she was little. It was a sister thing. No one else got to call her that. The nickname reminded her of an overeager puppy and was especially ridiculous for a dancer who actually danced jazz. Jazzy jazz dances. So stupid. The most irritating thing about Will was this—the madder she got, the quieter he got. And smirkier. If that was a thing. He was definitely smirky.

Brian had neglected to mention Will was taking over his orthodontic practice in Clover Park. She should've asked, in retrospect, but she'd been so excited about her new dance studio plans, the space next door was the last thing on her mind. Besides, last she'd heard, Will worked at a busy practice with three other orthodontists in a town about a half hour away. His office had been closed for a summer vacation during her three weeks of renovation.

She exhaled sharply. Being neighbors with Will was not going to be easy. She couldn't believe the fuss he made over the music. Obviously a dance studio needed music! She'd stand her ground. She never backed down from confrontation. And she never gave up. That was something the dance world had taught her—to be tough and keep pushing forward no matter what. She'd learned the hard way to keep a protective shell around her true feelings to shield herself from the sometimes hurtful critiques at auditions—too big of a head, too big butt, too curly hair—and show up bright and smiling at the next audition. Her fuck-them-all attitude allowed her to continue working relatively unscarred for years.

She settled at her small kitchen table and ate in front of her laptop, where she checked eLoveMatch, the online dating site she'd signed up for impulsively last week. She hadn't told a soul about it. She was a little embarrassed to be twenty-nine and hoping to find love for the first time. Well, there had been that one time, but, as she'd painfully discovered, that love had turned out to be all in her head. Anyway, she'd been too busy with her exhausting schedule of dance and auditions to worry about her lack of a love life. Sure, she'd had boyfriends here and there, mostly drawn from the tiny percentage of male dancers that were straight, and the occasional actor. But that never lasted more than a few weeks.

She'd started thinking about all this love stuff after she'd witnessed her friends Bare and Amber fall in love this summer right in front of the entire cast and crew's eyes. It was a palpable thing in the air. Now they were engaged to be married and deliriously happy.

She had several potential candidates in her inbox. Oh, look, older gentleman seeking companion in her twenties. The picture of a white-haired man in a muscle shirt standing next to a red Ferrari screamed trophy wife. Next, grandpa!

Adventurous male seeking female open to new experiences. That could be anything. Mountain biking or a sex club. Next!

Hardworking professional seeking the same. Oral hygiene a must. Her mind immediately flew to Will. Only an orthodontist or dentist would put oral hygiene at the top of the list. Adrenaline rushed through her. She clicked on it. Nope. Someone named Anthony.

She leaned back and sighed. She was *not* disappointed. She'd only been eager to tease Will about his profile. Despite the challenge he presented as a man in desperate need of loosening up, he was all wrong for her. He was uptight, rigid, a total rule follower. The man wore a freaking bow tie. Okay, yeah, his hair was a little wild, dark brown and sort of sticking up on top like he couldn't control its thickness. She felt herself flush. Holy cow, why was she thinking of Will's thickness? It'd been too long if she was actually thinking about what he had going on under those pressed trousers. Again.

She deleted her account, glad she'd never told anyone about her weak moment of loneliness.

~ ~ ~

Jasmine went to work eagerly the next afternoon for her two after-school classes. Clover Park had a lot of families, and word had gotten around that a former Broadway dancer was the instructor. Of course, most people in town knew her already. She'd grown up here.

Today she'd teach jazz and hip-hop, so she left her hair down in its wild curls. She liked to whip her hair around with certain dance styles. She did her usual stretches, remembering how Will had spied on her yesterday. She wondered if he'd show up again today.

The music wasn't too loud, quieter than yesterday anyway. She turned and stretched, facing the windows of the waiting room. No Will. Good. She didn't need to start every day with a fight. She finished stretching and danced just for the hell of it, lost in the music and the joy at the freedom of movement as energy flowed through her body. She danced a few more songs, then set up for the jazz class.

A short while later, cars started pulling up and parking out front. Some went around back. She had fifteen girls signed up in the eight-to-twelve-year-old class. She bounced on the balls of her feet. This was going to be awesome. She welcomed each girl, introduced herself to their parent, and invited them to stay in the small waiting room, where she'd left some magazines and several chairs.

The girls were eager to learn, some of them were in awe, remembering her from when she'd danced in *The Lion King* last year. A lot of families in town had come to the city to watch her in that family-friendly production. She finished the class an hour later and snagged her water to rehydrate. Her next class started in fifteen minutes.

She heard the chime that indicated the studio door had opened. Guess some students had shown up early. She headed to the waiting room to greet them and stopped short at the sight of Will standing there, looking aggravated. His hair was even wilder today, like he'd stuck both hands in it and pulled. He wore a white coat with his name embroidered over one pocket, Dr. Levi, D.D.S. A yellow bow tie peeked out the top of the buttoned-up coat.

She grinned. "Here for the hip-hop class, I assume?"

A muscle ticked in his jaw. He was pissed about something. This should be good.

"We need to talk about the parking situation," he said through clenched teeth.

The man needed a drink or a massage or to get laid or something. Her cheeks warmed. She wasn't going to help him with any of the above.

She lifted her hair off the back of her neck to cool it. "I parked in my reserved spot."

He stared at her neck. He did that a lot. Staring. She didn't know why because it always seemed to make him madder.

He glowered at her. "I have patients that need to park in this lot. You can't hog all the spaces for your classes. You need to ask the parents to form an orderly line for drop off and pick up."

"Oh, I do, huh?"

"Yes, you do."

"Is that what the yoga studio did?" Her dance studio had previously been a yoga studio.

He stared at her legs in tights that ended at the ankle; then his gaze fixated on her bare ankles. He spoke slowly. "I wasn't here when they were open, but I have to assume they found street parking. Otherwise, my dad would've mentioned it as a potential problem to me."

She shrugged. "Sometimes the parents like to stay to watch class. I mean, seriously, how many parking spaces do you really need? You can only work on one mouth at a time."

His head jerked back up to look in her eyes. "Just don't let them park out front," he ground out. He was going to whittle his teeth down to little stubs if he didn't stop clenching and grinding them. She felt it only fair to point that out to a man obsessed with teeth.

"You should loosen up your jaw," she said. "You're going to do some serious dental damage."

"Oh, that's rich." He shoved both hands in his hair and pulled. His hair stayed all wild, sticking out every which way. It was a little unsettling the way it made him look less uptight and more her kind of guy. "I put in four years at dental school, three years of graduate work in orthodontics, and *you're* telling *me* about dentistry."

She flashed a smile. "I keep my jaw nice and loose. Look at these choppers." She opened her mouth with a wide grin. She expected him to get madder and quieter, but instead he approached her.

She took a step back. He moved with her, and his hand cupped her jaw.

"Open," he said.

Her heart picked up speed. "Will, I'm not your patient." His hand was warm and firm. She should hate his touch, should pull away, but she found herself frozen. He'd never touched her before. Never been this close. He had this warm, spicy scent that wrapped itself around her.

He stared at her mouth. "I want to see your choppers."

This was weird, she thought even as she opened her mouth. He stared, very seriously.

"Bite," he said.

She clamped her teeth together in a bite. His warm finger stroked her jaw as he murmured, "A perfect bite. My father's work?"

She met his brown eyes, startled at the fire burning in them through his glasses. "Yes."

He nodded once before his gaze dropped to her mouth. She was having trouble forming a coherent thought as his warm hand now cupped her cheek.

"Jaz?" he asked before he slowly dipped his head.

"Yes?" she breathed, her heart hammering furiously.

"Dr. Will! There you are!" a voice boomed.

CHAPTER THREE

Jasmine was torn between disappointment and relief when Will jerked away from her. No, it was definitely relief, she told herself. She had no idea how that near-kiss had happened. One minute they were fighting, the next minute she was getting a dental exam, and then BOOM—weirdness. She glanced at Will, who looked as surprised as she was. He turned to the man in a white dentist coat standing in the doorway. "What is it?"

"I wanted to get your opinion on an unusual crossbite." The man—tall, lean, with wavy dark brown hair, and a big smile—crossed to her and pumped her hand. "Hi, I'm Tony Russo. *Doctor* Tony Russo."

"Jasmine Davis," she said.

He kept holding her hand and smiling at her. "You look so familiar. Have we met?"

He looked familiar too. She pulled her hand away. "Um…I'm not sure. Are you from around here?"

"No. I just recently moved here from the city."

"Oh. You might have seen me in a show. Do you like theater?"

He snapped his fingers. "It's that hair. You're Flirtygirl29, right? On eLovematch. I replied to your profile."

Jasmine's stomach dropped. Shit. Tony must've been the Anthony that felt oral hygiene was a must. Her cheeks burned. "No, that's not me."

"Yeah, on eLoveMatch." Tony turned to Will. "The dancer." He looked around. "I can't believe you're right next door."

Will smirked. "You're flirty girl?"

Jasmine crossed her arms. "You must be mistaken. I'm not on eLovematch."

Tony shook his head. "If you're not, then you've got a doppelganger. I'll go look it up on my laptop. You've got to see this."

He left.

Will smirked some more. "Looking for a love match, are we?"

"That was *not* me."

"Fighting girl would've been more accurate. Are you twenty-nine?"

She held up her hand. "I'm done talking about this. Tony is mistaken. You can check the website yourself." Thank goodness she'd deleted her account.

"I'd like to see you flirting," Will said. "Sure beats your major attitude."

She put her hands on her hips. "I'm not flirty girl!"

He just stood there, smirking at her. He was just loving this, Mr. Smirks-a-lot.

"I'm not!"

He broke out into a wide smile that she'd never seen on him. He almost looked…appealing. "Me thinks flirty girl protests too much."

A few students arrived. Thank goodness. She turned away from him and greeted her students. "Welcome, I'm Jasmine. I'm so happy to see you." She greeted the parents and guided the girls inside.

"We'll talk more about the parking situation later," Will called over the chattering girls.

"There is no situation," she sang with a big smile.

"So long, flirty!" he called with a wave.

She longed to yell at him, but couldn't with all her students there. Finally, he was out the door. Irritating, completely unappealing, smirky man.

~ ~ ~

For once Will was thankful for Tony's intrusion in his life. He'd been taken in by Jasmine's perfect bite and nearly crossed the line with her. That would've been a mistake. He did not need another aggravation in his life. Tony hadn't found Jasmine's profile on the dating website, but Will could tell she knew exactly what Tony was talking about. She probably deleted her account in a fit of temper over some imagined slight from a potential suitor. That sounded more like the Jasmine he knew. So touchy, so quick to fly off the handle. Though, he had to admit, the fact that Jasmine had turned to online dating was surprising. He would've thought she'd have no problem attracting a man. If you were the kind of guy who liked graceful dancers with long necks, wild hair, glowing skin, and a perfect bite. Not to mention her perky breasts, toned body, long legs, and swe-ee-eet ass. He got hard just thinking about it. He blew out a breath. It had been too long if he was even considering for one minute the possibility of some kind of physical…No. Absolutely not.

He assisted Tony with the crossbite. It was unusual in the way the lower jaw jutted out ahead of the upper, though the molars were in perfect alignment. He'd seen it once before and took the time to explain to Tony, the patient, and the boy's mother the recommended course of treatment with a night brace and mouthpiece.

A half hour later, Mrs. Parks, the mother of twin girl patients, remarked that she had to park a block away.

"What is going on?" Mrs. Parks asked. "Some kind

of special event?"

His blood pressure rose. He needed to hammer out an agreement with Jasmine over parking. He couldn't have his patients parking a block away. Let Jasmine's students park a block away. They were there to get exercise anyway.

"It's the new dance studio," he said. "Don't worry. It won't happen again."

"Oh, yes, I heard Jasmine opened it. Did you know her mother was in *Eye on Top*? You know, that spy movie."

He knew very little about Jasmine, other than that she was the bane of his existence. "No."

"She was Brock's girlfriend."

"Oh." That explained Jasmine's looks. He hadn't known her mother was an actress, though he knew her dad's band, The Davis Trio, had been the house band for a late-night talk show, *The Pete Macauley Show*. His dad was a big fan of the show before it went off the air.

As soon as he finished work, he stopped by Jasmine's dance studio for the sole purpose of straightening out the parking situation. Closed. He checked the back lot. Her car was still parked in her spot. That meant she was home. He knew she'd rented the apartment above the studio because when he'd called his dad last night to bitch about the fact that he'd rented the studio space to the very woman Will had fought with all summer, his dad had told him he rented her the apartment too. Will hadn't told his dad about all the fighting last summer, so it was all a big, hearty *ha-ha-ha* surprise to him. Will was not amused.

He had a quick debate over whether or not to knock on her apartment door or wait until the morning when he heard music blasting from upstairs. His blood pressure rose. What if he had evening patients as he did on Tuesday nights? It was Wednesday, but still. This music was way too loud. The two of them needed to get a few things straight.

He marched up the back staircase and pounded on the door so she'd hear him over that racket. The door opened. She stood there in a blue tank top and white and blue polka-dotted leggings. His gaze caught on her teddy bear slippers. Each cuddly teddy bear head wore a red bow tie. He was so shocked that Jasmine of all people liked cute bears wearing bow ties that he didn't even try to speak over the hip-hop music assaulting his ears.

"Need another look at these choppers, Dr. Levi?" she asked.

He tore his gaze from the slippers and stared at her bare shoulder. The strap of her tank top had slipped off her shoulder. There was no bra strap. He stared at her chest. Her nipples turned into points right under his very eyes. His mouth went dry. He couldn't remember why he'd shown up at her door.

She crossed her arms over her chest. "Eyes up here," she snapped.

He blinked and finally met her eyes. "Your music's too loud."

"What?"

"I said your music's too loud!" he shouted over the music.

She put a hand to her ear. "What?"

She was making a joke at his expense. Again. He pushed past her, located the offending speaker dock, and turned down the music.

"What the hell do you think you're doing?" she hollered. "You come into my apartment and turn down my music? Uh-uh. No way. No how. Get out!"

"What are you wearing?" He stared at her polka-dotted leggings. He'd never seen her wear polka dots before. It was so cute and un-Jasmine-like.

She exhaled noisily. "I'm wearing my pajamas because it's after dinner, and I planned on staying in. Now, if you don't have any more asinine questions, goodbye!"

She turned and went to the speaker dock, cranking the music up even louder than before. She headed to the small kitchen. He followed her.

"What?" she hollered. "Why are you still here?"

"We need to talk," he said quietly.

"What? I can't hear you over the music." She shrugged and reached on tiptoe for a wineglass from the cabinet. He did *not* stare at her bare lower back as the tank top lifted or her sweet ass revealed through the tight leggings because he was there on a mission. She poured herself a glass of wine, sipped, and watched him over the rim of the glass.

She gestured to the wine, offering him some. He slowly shook his head no. He hadn't had a drink in thirteen years. Lucky thirteen.

She rolled her eyes before heading back to the living room to turn down the music. She sat on a black leather sofa and tucked a leg under her. "Sit!"

He sat. He made sure she wasn't in arm's reach, that way he wouldn't be tempted by her perfect bite again.

She raised her brows and stared at him expectantly. "So what crawled up your ass and died this time?"

He ignored her barbed comment. He didn't come here to fight. "We need to work out an agreement over the shared use of the building."

"I signed a lease with your dad. That was my agreement."

"I mean the music. I think we should agree on a decibel level."

A ghost of a smile crossed her face that she quickly

covered by taking a long drink of wine. "What decibel level would you like?"

"I think fifty would be appropriate."

"Done," she said.

"Really?"

"Really!" she mocked in a high pitch. He did *not* sound like that when he was excited. "Fifty decibels could be exactly where I have it for all I know." She snorted. "Decibels."

He ground his teeth. "I can put a piece of tape where it would be."

She narrowed her eyes. "You'd better move off this topic before you really piss me off."

They had a stare down that had his mind wandering back to the fact that she wore no bra. He looked away first, not liking where his mind was going. They were alone in her apartment. She wore the thinnest of pajamas with no bra. He couldn't help but wonder what she tasted like. Probably fruity with a hint of spice, like her scent. Or maybe that was her shampoo or body wash or something. *Get a hold of yourself! Jasmine is nothing but more aggravation and trouble for you.*

He met her eyes and could tell she was trying not to smile, which irked him. She did *not* win that stare down. It was all the bra's fault. It should've been on her. That was an unfair distraction.

He took a deep breath in and out. He had to bring

the conversation back to the building and its uses. His gaze caught on her breasts. They seemed to like him. They came to attention whenever he stared at them.

"Is my chest bothering you?" she asked. "Should I turn it down too?"

He couldn't answer because her breasts were like high beams, and he was caught in them.

"You won't win, you know," she said.

Will scrunched up his brows, suddenly wary. "Win what?"

"You won't get your way just by trying to make me uncomfortable. I'm not embarrassed that easily. I performed for a living." She raised her chin. "I danced topless in *Hair*."

Now that was too much. She'd turned the tables and was trying to make him uncomfortable and distracted and painfully hard. He would not lose this fight. Were they fighting? He stared at her mouth, where a small smile played over her lips.

"I don't believe you," he said. "You would never dance topless." He hoped the challenge would make her want to show him that she could. *Yeah, Jaz, show me. Put me in my place.* "You're much too uptight for that," he added, trying very hard not to laugh.

She sputtered. "I'm uptight? Are you kidding me?" She narrowed her eyes. "You're trying to make me mad."

"And you're trying to flaunt your sexy body to get your way."

She picked up her wineglass and took a sip, watching him over the rim. "You think I'm sexy?"

He snorted. "It's pretty obvious."

"Thank you," she said softly.

He'd never heard a soft voice come out of that mouth. He scooted closer. Just one taste. Honest. She had such a perfect bite. He also had a perfect bite, which meant they would fit together perfectly. He just wanted to test that theory—

"What are you doing?" she asked in an alarmed voice.

He wanted the soft voice back. He pushed her hair over her shoulder. "What do you think I'm doing?"

"Will," she said shakily.

One corner of his mouth lifted. "Your voice is shaking." Was she that affected by him?

She crossed her arms. "It is not," she protested hotly.

"Am I making you nervous?"

She licked her lips, which hit him right where it counted. Just a taste.

"You do *not* make me nervous." She stood abruptly. "You should go."

Dammit. He shouldn't have mentioned her shaking voice. He studied her for a moment, all tense and working up to a good mad. "I'm sorry I made you uncomfortable." He patted the sofa. "Sit down. I just want to talk to you about the building."

"No."

"Are you too scared to sit next to me?"

She immediately sat next to him again. He knew she couldn't resist that challenge, calling her chicken. But now she was all stiff and closed against him. Her arms were crossed as she stared straight ahead.

A few moments passed in silence while he considered his next move. He admitted reluctantly to himself that her message was loud and clear. She didn't want him. If she did, she would've stayed all soft voiced and let him test his perfect-bite theory. Might as well address the whole reason he'd come here in the first place. He'd gotten distracted by the pajamas. He was sure any guy looking at her in those pajamas would've had the same reaction.

"We need to discuss parking," he said.

She let out a big sigh like he was super annoying. That didn't change the facts. The parking situation was completely out of hand.

"I told you the parents like to stick around," she said with a bit of an edge to her voice that immediately set him on edge.

"Mrs. Parks had to park a block away," he said, working hard to keep his voice level and calm.

"Mrs. Parks parks," she said in a singsong voice.

His blood pressure went through the roof. "I'm serious!"

Her eyes flashed. "Look, *William*, I have a lot of young students with driving parents. They will park out front. They will park out back. And if you have a problem with that, I suggest you take it up with your dad, who owns the building."

"No, you look, *Jazzy*." She glared at him and that just spurred him on. Sexy pajamas or not, he was in the right here. "I also have a lot of young patients with driving parents. They will not be forced to park a block away." She sipped her wine casually, but he saw the challenge in her eyes. She would not best him. "I think an equitable division of parking spaces is sixty-forty, given the size of your classes."

"Eighty-twenty," she fired back.

"Seventy-five, twenty-five," he shot back.

"Ninety-ten," she said, setting down her wineglass and glaring at him.

"You're impossible!" He stood in his aggravation. Everything with Jasmine was one big frustration. "There's no reasoning with you!"

"You need a chill pill. Seriously. You have until the count of three to get out of my apartment before I kick your ass."

"I'm not afraid of you."

She stood and went toe-to-toe with him. "You should be."

Her scent wrapped around him. He couldn't move. His gaze dropped to her mouth. Her lips, full and ripe, her perfect bite. He searched for a snappy comeback to really put her in her place, but what came out was, "I have a perfect bite too."

She jabbed a finger in his chest. "Do *not* speak orthodontist to me."

"Jaz," he said in what he hoped was a coaxing voice.

"One," she said. When he didn't move, she added, "I'll call the cops. Two."

"This isn't over," he snapped before heading for the door.

"I'm shaking in my slippers!" she hollered after him.

He slammed the door behind him, not that she'd notice because the music was already blasting. Everything with that woman was all-out war. She needed to get in touch with her softer side, if such a thing even existed. He thought again of her cute teddy bear slippers. Of that one moment when she'd spoken softly, when her voice had gotten shaky. Maybe she did have a softer side. She just tried to hide it from the world.

He was too aggravated to go home and found

himself walking toward Main Street a block away. The sign from Garner's Sports Bar & Grill glowed, beckoning him in. One drink. He was so wound up. He needed to relax somehow. He headed in, stared at the bar, and lingered in the lobby, where he pretended to be studying a bulletin board covered in local flyers while he debated getting that drink. He was clean and straight as an arrow ever since the car accident that had landed his older brother, Charlie, in a coma. Will had been at the wheel, stoned out of his mind.

He and Charlie had been home on break from college for the holidays. Will had been a sophomore pulling Bs and Cs. Charlie had been a senior with straight As, already accepted to a prestigious dental school. Charlie had been at a party and, being the responsible one, realized he'd had too many drinks and called home for a ride. Will answered the phone, already stoned after hanging out at his friend's house, and offered to go. It was only a twenty-minute drive, he'd figured. What could happen? His parents had already been asleep.

He made it there no problem. Halfway back, he'd been laughing and joking around, not noticing the red light. He swerved to avoid an oncoming car, hit a patch of ice, spun out, and slammed into a tree. The impact was on the passenger side. The airbag deployed, and his brother was unconscious with blood trickling down his head. Will had been afraid to touch him, unsure how bad the damage was. Will was completely uninjured.

It was his fault. All his fault. The refrain ran on repeat through his head as he rode with Charlie in the ambulance. As he stayed with him in the hospital, where Charlie was in a coma. As he had to explain everything to their parents. Those three days before Charlie woke were utter hell. His parents blamed him. Will could do nothing, absolutely nothing to fix things.

Then Charlie woke. His parents forgave Will. That should've been enough, but it wasn't because Will couldn't forgive himself. He watched his brother recover from surgery on his damaged right leg, sweat through physical therapy, deal with the pain of the injury that left him not quite whole. And once Charlie was back on his feet, still using a cane, he'd changed. He was Chaz the wanderer, the pothead, the guy who didn't care about anything—not home, not dental school, not working. Nothing.

Will stepped up in his place. He dropped his vices—no drugs, no alcohol, no more partying, ever. He worked hard to bring up his grades and applied for the very same dental school Charlie had planned on going to. He went onto orthodontics, intent on taking over the family business. He'd pleased his father, made up for his brother, and eventually came to like the work because of the results. He boosted the health and confidence of his patients, helping them to have a perfect smile.

But every time he thought of his brother walking with a cane, driving a special van with hand controls instead of pedals, parking in the handicapped space, the guilt damn near killed him. It should've been Will who suffered. His never-ending guilt was like a straitjacket, forcing him to make up for his wrongdoing by living life by the rules.

He blew out a breath, deciding he'd skip the drink. He didn't deserve any relief. His eye caught on a flyer with bold letters proclaiming Relaxation Guaranteed. He got closer to read the fine print. It was a knitting club. The flyer said all levels and all ages welcome. He snorted. Knitting was for girls. He turned away, heading out the door.

When he got home, Sweetie met him at the door. He reached down to stroke the gray cat's head. Sweetie hissed, showing sharp incisors. Will withdrew his hand and straightened, strangely hurt by the rejection.

Maybe he should join that knitting club just to meet someone. It did say all ages were welcome. Maybe there would be someone his age there willing to have sex with him. That would definitely relax him. Guaranteed. It'd been a while. Eight months to be exact, ever since his girlfriend of two years, Carrie, dumped him. That too had felt like some weird cosmic retribution because Carrie had dumped him for his brother, Chaz.

The betrayal had cut deep. He'd loved her, had hoped to marry her. They'd flown out to California to visit Chaz over the New Year. Carrie stayed because, as she said, Chaz was more fun. Despite all the horrible bitterness rotting Will's heart, a few months later, when it became apparent that his brother was happy and the two of them were madly in love, Will forgave Chaz.

Mostly because Will knew, deep down, he deserved whatever shit life threw his way.

CHAPTER FOUR

After a week of fighting with Will over the music volume and parking, which Jasmine had to admit had become fun because he was so predictable in his responses (her favorite was the hair-tugging wild-man look), she decided it was time to change things up a bit. As much as she liked watching Will get worked up, it would make both of their lives a little easier if the man would just lighten up.

She decided to email him jokes. It was silly and off-the-wall and exactly what he wouldn't be expecting. She giggled to herself, imagining him puzzling over a corny joke. She'd love to see him smile more. He had a really nice smile. Certainly better than his scowl, or his unnerving stare at various parts of her body that embarrassingly came to attention under his gaze.

On Monday morning, she headed to the reception area of his office, introduced herself to the receptionist,

Hillary, and took a business card.

"Is this the best email to reach Tony?" she asked.

Hillary gestured for the card. Jasmine handed it back and watched as Hillary wrote his email on the back. "This is the one we use for him. The other is for general inquiries. I'm the one who answers that one."

Jasmine grinned. "Great! Thanks so much, Hillary."

"No problem," Hillary chirped.

Jasmine headed back to her apartment, smiling to herself. The email address was simple: DrRusso at LeviOrthodontics. She was sure Will's email address would be similar. She went to her laptop and opened a new email account to keep her identity a secret. He wouldn't think it was funny if it was coming from her. She went with Glamstick since Will was such a stick in the mud and quickly typed:

Dear Dr. Levi,

What does an orthodontist do during an earthquake?

He braces himself. :p

From,

Your BIGGEST Fan

She checked back a little later to see if the email bounced. It didn't. That meant she'd guessed his email address right. Maybe next time she'd send him a dirty joke. She could just imagine the look on his face when he opened that one.

~ ~ ~

Will ate lunch at his desk and checked his email. That was odd. An email from Glamstick. He was about to delete it when the subject line made him curious— Important Orthodontic News. Huh. Maybe it was a new product. He got those sometimes. He clicked on the message. He scrunched his brows reading the strange email. A corny joke? His biggest fan? Sounded like one of his teenaged patients. Just what he needed to add more stress and aggravation to his life—an underage girl with a crush on him sending inappropriate emails. He deleted it and hoped that was the end of it.

He stood, thinking a walk in the fresh air might help lessen his aggravation.

Tony darkened his doorway. "Hey, Dr. Will."

"Hello, Dr. Russo. What can I help you with?"

Tony grinned. "Hillary says Jasmine asked for my email."

Will stiffened.

"You think she'd go out with me?"

Will wasn't sure how to answer. A yes would encourage Tony. What if Tony and Jasmine started dating? Will would have to watch her perfect bite on Tony's perfect bite on a regular basis. A no would also encourage Tony. The man had his own ridiculous agenda. Just today Tony had brought his pet iguana in, saying that patients would enjoy feeding it crickets before their appointments. Will had sent the offending thing home immediately. There was no right answer with Tony.

"I don't know," Will finally said. "But I have to warn you, she's a difficult woman. I found her impossible to work with this past summer at the community theater."

Tony rubbed his hands together. "I like a challenge. And, in case you hadn't noticed, she's supermodel hot."

Will cleared his throat. "She's too short to be a supermodel. I'm heading out for a walk."

"Great! I'll join you."

Will stifled a groan. He wanted a break from the people who aggravated him, not more aggravation.

"So, what's she like?" Tony asked eagerly. "Give me the inside scoop."

Will walked quickly past the front of Jasmine's dance studio, not wanting to risk a look at her in another skintight dancing outfit. She favored leotards and tights that ended at the ankle with ballet shoes. Sometimes she had her hair up tight in a bun, but sometimes it was loose and wild, which was much harder to ignore.

"She's like a snapping crocodile," Will said. "Get too close, and she'll bite your head off." He glanced at Tony. "Or another significant part," he added ominously.

Tony laughed heartily. "Sounds like you're afraid of her."

Will snorted. "More like extremely aggravated."

"I think she could be a lot of fun, know what I mean?" Tony elbowed him.

Will's hands formed fists. He stopped to face Tony and snarled, "Don't cross the line with her."

Tony's eyes widened. "Cool it, Doc. I'm just talking about having a good time. What kind of guy do you think I am?"

Will resumed walking, wishing he could lose Tony and just keep walking far, far away from everything that aggravated him. They walked in silence for a few minutes, heading toward Main Street. Will couldn't remember the last time he had a good time. Maybe when he'd gotten a hole-in-one, but it'd been a long time since that had happened. His golf game had gone steadily downhill since this past summer.

"Hey, I'm gonna grab a coffee," Tony said, gesturing toward Something's Brewing Café. "You want one?"

"No, thank you. I'll see you back at the office."

Tony saluted him and went inside. Will kept walking, taking a long, roundabout way back, needing the space to himself. It was none of his business if Tony asked Jasmine out. She'd probably say no anyway. He suspected Jasmine would go for someone more like herself—a free spirit. Someone loosey-goosey, like an artist or another dancer. Of course, Tony was a little out there. Maybe she'd like that. He could never tell about the mysterious man-woman stuff. Obviously, or he wouldn't have been blindsided by his brother and Carrie hooking up.

He headed back to the office. There was nothing he could do about Tony and Jasmine possibly getting together. Unless he fired Tony. The idea had merit. But then he'd be short-staffed, and the fact was, Tony knew his way around the dental orifice. No, it would be better to warn Jasmine off of Tony. That settled, Will went to work on his next patient.

After work, he went to Jasmine's dance studio, where he found her mopping the dance floor. "Don't you have someone to do that?" he asked.

"I have me, myself, and I," she replied. "It's not a big deal."

He watched her clean for a moment. The woman was even graceful doing a chore. She kept mopping, and he kept not watching her cleavage whenever she leaned forward.

She stopped and sighed heavily. "What do you want, Will?"

"I wanted to let you know that Tony can be quite aggravating on a one-on-one basis, and he favors exotic pets. As far as I know, he has an iguana, a tarantula, and a snake. He's very interested in capuchin monkeys as well."

She stared at him. "And your point is?"

"That was my point."

She shook her head and went back to mopping, ignoring him. He kept not watching her.

She looked up. "Bye, Will."

He took the hint. "Bye, Jasmine."

~ ~ ~

Will went home that night and decided the best way to deal with Jasmine was at a distance. He drafted an email memo to the occupants of building 101, which consisted of him and his staff and Jasmine. He detailed the number of parking spaces in the front and back of the building and exactly who should park where. He went to pull Jasmine's email address from her Clover Park Dance Studio website and got distracted.

She'd attended the Manhattan Performing Arts High School with a major in dance and had appeared in many well-known Broadway and off-Broadway shows. He'd seen *Chicago* with his family five years ago on Broadway, which was one of her credits. Maybe he'd seen her perform before they'd officially met. He lingered over the picture of her smiling, looking right at the camera. She so rarely smiled at him, which was a very good thing, because she was magnificent. He didn't want to be blinded by her beauty only to fall prey to her sharp claws and snarling demeanor.

He cc'd his dad on the email should Jasmine have any doubt that he was, in fact, in touch with the landlord over such an important issue. His dad's immediate reply that parking had always been first-come, first-serve was not at all helpful, so Will replied with a second email that did not include his dad that from now on, there would be exactly six spaces allocated to Levi Orthodontics in the back parking lot and the remaining ten parking spaces would be allocated to the Clover Park Dance Studio. It was the sixty-forty split he'd first brought up with her, and he thought it more than fair. He decided on the spot to hire a painting company to number the spaces and added that bit in. Reserved spaces would remain the same. Any overflow would need to find street parking.

He checked his email before bed in case Jasmine had some response to his memo and was disheartened to find another email from Glamstick. Again the subject line was: Important Orthodontic News. He clicked on it. It was a picture of two cats battling with light sabers. The caption said, "The force is strong with you, young kitty."

Will was not amused. The last thing he needed was some angry parent spreading the word that he was inappropriate with a patient. He replied to the email: *Who are you? How old are you? I will find out if you don't tell me. I can track email addresses.*

That last part wasn't true, but he thought it sounded just strong enough to discourage a teenage girl in her folly.

No reply. Good. Problem solved.

~ ~ ~

Over the next three weeks, Jasmine got into a nice routine—teach dance, work on marketing to increase business, and drive Will nuts by ignoring his numbered parking system and playing music that was not really all that loud, but definitely above his mandated fifty decibels, whatever that was. She'd stopped sending him funny emails because he wasn't lightening up at all. It had been a silly thing to do in any case.

Tony stopped by frequently to chat. He was a nice guy, always very interested in her dance studio. When she told him she was considering starting an adult tap class, he declared he'd be the first to sign up for it.

Then he said he'd recruit for her from the moms that came into the office. Next thing you knew, she had twenty students in her new Tuesday night class. Tony rocked.

The first night of class was a smashing success. Tony was a bit heavy footed, but more than made up for it in enthusiasm. The women loved having him in class, as he was always joking around. The best part was how her students really took to tap. She kept throwing out more moves, and they kept up.

She finished the class and sent everyone off with a smile. She cleaned up the studio and headed out to the waiting room to straighten up. Tony was still there.

"Oh, hi, Tony. Great class tonight."

"You were awesome. I had a lot of fun."

"Good."

The door opened and a sour-faced Will came in.

"You just missed the best tap class, Dr. Will," Tony said.

"May I speak with you privately?" Will asked Jasmine.

"See ya later," Tony said before he leaned over and gave Jasmine a quick kiss on the cheek.

"Bye!" Jasmine said with a smile. She was used to the kissy hello and goodbye. Theater people were very touchy-feely.

Will stood there, glowering at her. She stared back

at him, waiting for whatever pissed him off this time.

"Did Tony ask you out?" he demanded.

"No." She studied him. "Why?"

He looked out the front window and turned back. "Your tap class coincides with my late office hours on Tuesdays."

"Okay." She stacked some magazines neatly back in the magazine rack.

"So it's very noisy over here."

She ignored him. The man was obsessed with noise. It was tap. It was supposed to be noisy. In a rhythmic way.

He cleared his throat. "It sounds like a herd of hippos."

"It's tap," she said, offended that he compared her enthusiastic students to hippos. Okay, no one was graceful at their first lesson, but given time they could really come along. She was already thinking about having a special performance with the adults to show her younger students how far you could take tap.

"How long will you be holding this Tuesday evening class?" he asked.

"At least until the end of the year. That's how long they signed up for." She looked around the small waiting room. Everything seemed in order. She headed for the door.

"Where are you going?" Will demanded, blocking

her way and standing too close. He smelled delicious, spicy and masculine, and she was way too tempted. "We're not done talking."

She lifted her chin. "I'm done."

"We have a problem," he said. And she wasn't sure which problem he was referring to—the noise or the fact that whenever they got close, there was a sizzling tension in the air. He was staring at her mouth again.

She was starting to feel panicky with Will blocking the door and standing so close. She was sure she was a mess after sweating through so many dance classes. Her hair was a crazy tangle, for sure. And besides all that, she should never get involved with someone she wanted to strangle half the time. She glanced down, noticed the bulge, and swallowed hard.

"You're in my way," she said, but what she really meant was *just kiss me and get it over with*. Will didn't get that message. Instead, he spoke in an arrogant, challenging voice that had her temper flaring.

"So make me move."

She shoved him with both hands on his chest, and he merely snagged her wrists. She'd walked right into that one. "Let go," she said softly, not really meaning it.

"I'm not done talking." He was still staring at her mouth, which irritated her beyond belief. Either kiss her or don't kiss her, but stop teasing her like this with all this closeness and stuff. He still hadn't made a move one excruciatingly long tension-filled moment later, so she yanked her hands free.

She darted around him, opened the door, and waited for him to go out ahead of her. She locked the door behind her and was about to walk down the hallway to the back door that led to her apartment when Will snagged her elbow.

"What?" she asked, completely exasperated with all his confusing touches.

He let go. "I have a solution. Rather than fight with you every Tuesday night over an insane amount of tapping and loud music while I'm trying to work, you could simply soundproof the wall on your side of the building."

Just what she needed—another expense for her new business. She was already in debt up to her eyeballs from the loan she'd taken out to get it started.

She put her hands on her hips and glared at him. "You could simply soundproof the wall on your side of the building!"

"But I'm not the one creating a ruckus," he said calmly.

"A ruckus?" she barked. "Okay, here's how it's going to be. You have two choices. One. Change your evening hours—"

"Impossible. They're already set for the next three

months."

"Two. Soundproof your side of the building."

"Tony's the loudest one there, isn't he? Maybe you should kick him out."

She narrowed her eyes. "What is it with you and Tony? He's not the loudest one." Actually, he was. If anyone was the hippo in class, it was Tony. "He's a fabulous dancer. I was impressed. Very light on his feet."

Will snorted. "Twinkle toes."

Jasmine did a head swivel, turned on her heel, and headed to her apartment. There was no point in arguing with Will. It was a never-ending ride on the carousel of crazy.

"This town has noise ordinances!" he called.

She kept walking, but still snapped her fingers and thumb together in a gesture of *blah, blah, blah* to him.

"Jazzy!" he mocked in a last-ditch attempt to rile her. "Flirty girl!"

She made a less friendly hand gesture. She heard a thump like he'd kicked the wall. She shook her head and went upstairs. After a long shower, she settled on the sofa with a glass of wine and her laptop. She sent an email to Will from Glamstick because she was still pissed and couldn't get him out of her head. *What's the opposite of a good time? Answer: An appointment with an orthodontist.* She hit send and grinned.

An email dinged back a few minutes later. *Who is this? How old are you?*

She stared at the words. Did she want to engage? Would he just piss her off via email?

Another email came in. *Are you female? I want answers.*

She took a fortifying drink of wine. Well, the whole point of her emails had been to loosen him up, so here we go.

She replied: *I'm female, over eighteen, frisky, and fun.*

Me too. Except I'm male, but you know that, Frisky.

She snorted. *What's a dentist's favorite animal?* She waited and thought she'd lost him when he finally emailed back.

A monkey?

She giggled and emailed back. *Why would you say a monkey?*

Because it's a primate and genetically close to the human jaw and teeth formation.

She rolled her eyes. Frisky and fun? Not. She replied with the punchline: *A molar bear.*

Okay.

Are you laughing yourself silly?

Yes.

She smiled. *What do you do for fun?*

I waterski with molar bears.

She laughed out loud. He did have a sense of

humor!

What do you do for fun? he asked.

I flirt with orthodontists.

Lucky me.

Lucky you. Night, Dr. Levi.

Night, Frisky.

She quickly shut the laptop. That was very weird. She smiled to herself. She kinda liked weird.

~ ~ ~

"Congratulations, you guys!" Jasmine said when it was her turn to congratulate her friends Bare Furnukle and Amber Lewis-Furnukle on their newly married status. They were in the Clover Park mansion for their wedding and reception. The mansion had some historic name, but everyone in town called it that.

"Thank you!" Amber said, hugging her.

"So glad you could make it," Bare said, reaching down to give her a hug.

"Can't wait until the dancing starts," she said with a wink toward Amber. Her friend had asked for some Irish jig dancing lessons to surprise Bare at their wedding reception.

"Me too!" Bare said.

"See you in a bit," Amber said. The bride wore a pink wedding dress with pink tulle that perfectly matched the pink highlights in her hair.

Jasmine loved to shake things up a bit, but if it was her wedding, she'd be wearing that long white dress with a train that required two people to carry it. She headed over to the reception area where the cast and crew from *The Pirates of Penzance* had gathered around the bar. Bare and Amber had invited everyone from the community theater, which meant Will was around here somewhere. Not that she cared what he did.

She found her friend Steph. "Look at you, girl! I love your shoes." She gave Steph a hug, careful not to mess up her hair.

"Thanks," Steph said. "I love your dress!"

"Thanks, it's my little black dress." She loved this dress. It had an asymmetric top with only one strap over her shoulder; the other shoulder was bare.

"I'd like you to meet Dave," Steph said. "Dave, this is Jasmine. She was the choreographer for our show."

Dave, a mild-mannered guy with a conservative haircut and black-rimmed glasses, shook her hand. "Nice to meet you, Jasmine."

"It's so nice to finally meet you," she said. "Steph's been talking about the fabulous Dave Olsen for weeks!"

He blushed. "That's good, I hope."

"Absolutely!" Jasmine said. "Are you going to get out on the dance floor with Steph?"

"Sure," Dave said.

"A guy who dances," Jasmine said to Steph. "Hang onto that one."

Steph wrapped her arm around his. "Oh, I intend to."

A tuxedoed waiter stopped next to them with a tray full of champagne. She and Steph took one. She sipped, felt someone staring at her, and turned to see Will standing in the corner wearing a dark gray suit with a dark gray bow tie. He didn't have a date for the wedding. She met his gaze and held up her champagne in an ironic toast to him.

He crossed the room toward her. Oh, shit. The cut of the suit fit him perfectly. He sort of looked in shape and kind of muscular, which she'd never noticed under the dentist coat, okay, maybe this summer she'd noticed some muscular forearms, but—damn, it was hot in here.

"What are we toasting?" he asked when he reached her side.

She breathed in his spicy, deliciously masculine scent and tried to appear unaffected. "The happy couple," she chirped.

"Hi, Will," Steph said with a big smile. Her friend knew all about her feud with Will. Steph had played one of the Major-General's daughters in the play and seen them fighting this summer. And, of course, she'd kept Steph up to date on all of Will's ridiculous demands since they became neighbors.

"Hi, Steph," Will said with a warm smile. "Good to see you again."

Where was her warm smile from Will? All she got were scowls and stares out of him. She listened as Steph introduced Will to Dave. It turned out Will had grown up in the town where Dave now taught math and some of the same teachers were still at the middle school.

She chatted with Steph while Will talked to Dave, until they were all called into the reception area where the DJ had started the music. She dragged Steph out on the dance floor. Dave and Will watched. She really didn't care if Will watched her. He always watched her.

She danced and glanced at him, looking entirely too appealing in that suit, and quickly turned back to Steph. She knew how to get Will to stop staring. Just do some sexy move, and he'd turn away because he was way too uptight to handle that. She put her hands on her knees and did a low squat, followed by a booty roll, butt up first, the rest of her rolling on up.

He scowled and walked away.

Her night got a lot easier after that. She danced a ton of songs with the cast and crew from the play. Zac and Kevin had especially good rhythm, so she spent most of her time with them. Then she heard Bare holler, "I love you, wench!" and she turned to see both Bare and Amber doing an Irish jig.

Everyone on the dance floor backed up, letting the couple take center stage. She clapped along with everyone, proud of Amber for taking to the dance steps so well. After a little while, everyone else joined in, dancing the crazy jig with them.

"Ow!" Steph said on her right. Apparently, Dave had two left feet.

"Sorry!" Dave said for like the millionth time.

Jasmine shifted a little further from Dave. After that crazy song, a slow song started, and Jasmine headed to a table to rehydrate. This military guy came up and asked Amber's sister, Kate, to dance. Ian, Bare's brother, who had previously been sitting on the other side of the table, suddenly stood and appeared at Jasmine's side.

"Would you like to dance?" he asked.

"Sure," she said.

He led her onto the dance floor and stopped right next to Kate and the military guy.

"Nice wedding," she said.

He murmured something that sounded like mmm-hmm. He held her stiffly at a distance, and his head was turned so he could stare at Kate. She felt like rolling her eyes. What was this, a revenge dance?

"You want to switch partners?" she asked.

"Yes," he said, then dropped his hands and stopped in front of the other couple. The guy sent him away. Ian scowled and came back to her.

"Guess you're stuck with me," she said.

"My brother is an ass," he said.

"Bare? That's harsh to talk about the groom that way."

"No, him." He jerked his head in the direction of the military guy. "Daniel. Kate's mine. I was her first."

Omigod. He did *not* just say that.

"Look, Ian, you don't talk about your"—she lowered her voice—"sex life with another woman to someone like me that you barely know. I think we've met twice now. And especially not if you took her virginity. Geez!"

"I'm in love with her," he said morosely.

Jasmine sighed. Why did she always get stuck with such irritating guys? Like this guy or Will. Why couldn't she meet a nice guy like Bare? She looked around the dance floor, curious if Will would venture out for a slow dance. Most guys would do a slow dance, a rare few like Bare had the confidence to dance the fast dances. Nope. She found him standing in a corner. Alone.

Why didn't he socialize? Why did he keep standing in corners? It wasn't like he didn't know anyone here. As soon as the song ended, Ian went after Kate, and Jasmine headed toward Will.

"Having fun?" he asked when she got to his side.

"Why are you standing in the corner?"

"It's quieter over here away from the DJ," he responded.

Just then the DJ blasted "Saturday Night Fever" by the Bee Gees and a disco ball spun. Bare ran out on the dance floor, pulling Amber along. He immediately launched into a John Travolta impersonation.

Jasmine laughed and turned back to Will. "How come you don't dance?"

He looked at her with half-hooded eyes. "Disco's not my thing."

"Come on, this is fun," she said. "Look, the whole gang from this summer's out there. You know everyone."

"Are you asking me to dance, Jaz?" His voice was low and husky, half challenge, half invitation.

"No," she quickly said. "I was just wondering why you're like a lump on a log."

He stared out at the dance floor. "I'd rather watch everyone else dance."

She wrinkled her nose. "That's not very fun."

"Oh, it's fun." He smirked. He was such a smirky, smirky man. Then he added, "It's just like that chick flick…" He snapped his fingers. "What's it called again?"

"Um, *My Best Friend's Wedding*?"

"Sure. That one. Very romantic." He smirked again. "My heart's aflutter."

She huffed and turned to go.

"Did I insult your movie?"

She turned back. "I seriously think you don't know how to have fun."

He said nothing. Just stared straight ahead. He was such a stick in the mud, even at a wedding, she just wanted to shake him. Why was she wasting her time trying to talk to him?

"What do you do for fun?" she asked.

"I waterski with molar bears," he said with no trace of humor.

She stiffened. Omigod. Did he know it was her? But he was still staring straight ahead. Not acting like he knew it was her who'd emailed and joked with him. Why couldn't he be more like that guy in real life?

"What's that supposed to mean?" she asked.

He shook his head. "Nothing." He turned and stared at her bare shoulder. "Just a corny joke."

She relaxed again. "Well, have fun standing in the corner." She headed back to the dance floor.

"Oh, I will," he called. He always had to have the last word.

"I doubt it!" she hollered over her shoulder.

"You don't know corners like I do!" he hollered back.

She snorted and jumped in next to the wedding couple, doing some John Travolta moves of her own, knowing Will was watching. Uncomfortable, she turned her back to him and saw Steph doing some kind of pole dance on her boyfriend. *You go, girl!* She could just imagine Will's response if she did that to him. Hell, she should show him what an excellent pole he'd make—stiff and straight, completely inflexible, rigid.

*Rigid and thick…*She felt herself flush and peeked over her shoulder to find Will still staring at her.

He smiled at her unexpectedly and then gestured for her to continue like she was dancing just for him. That rare smile had her imagining a private dance, something slow and sexy, stripping as she went. She shook her head. She'd had way too much champagne if the idea of a striptease for Will was turning her on.

She tossed her hair and turned away.

~ ~ ~

Will was in a strange state of mind when he got ready for work on Monday morning. He'd spent entirely too much time watching Jasmine dance at Barry and Amber's wedding. He wanted to stop, but he couldn't tear himself away. He kept imagining her doing a sexy dance just for him, maybe some kind of striptease that didn't involve talking. Because the minute she opened her mouth, they were fighting.

What did he care anyway? He'd spent the last week corresponding with some unknown frisky female of legal age and found himself looking forward to their evening chat sessions. He thought maybe she was a bit of a recluse, or shy, or a computer nerd, and that's why she'd reached out to him through email, but he found he didn't care. He was enjoying their silly conversations and hoping one day to meet her.

Besides, Tony had a thing for Jasmine now. He'd spent the last week talking nonstop about how great she was and how he was definitely going to ask her out at the next tap class, which was more information than Will needed to know. Tony licked his lips incessantly when he talked about Jasmine, reminding Will of a hungry wolf. And did Tony have to blab about every single stinking thing going on in his life?

Things went downhill fast that morning. First, Sweetie ripped a hole in Will's best sweater (that he'd left on the dresser to take to the dry cleaner) and then threw up on it. When Will got to work he discovered that Tony had set up a video game system in the waiting room to entertain their patients. Even worse, Tony had bought the *Party Dance* video game and informed Will that Jasmine would be stopping by to play after hours. He did *not* need to see Jasmine dancing in his very own waiting room. Not after those sexy dance moves from the wedding were burned into his brain.

During work, his newest patient, a nine-year-old boy, bit him during the exam. Hard. That hurt like a mother. The boy hadn't apologized, and his mother had made an excuse for him, saying he was scared of the dentist. Will couldn't have been more gentle; he'd barely touched the kid. The day wore on and on as Will pondered, not for the first time, why he'd gotten into a profession where most of his patients dreaded seeing him. Sure, it was satisfying seeing the results of his work, but his patients had to be dragged in and were clearly not happy to be there.

Of course, he knew the real reason he'd gotten into the field—taking his brother's place while fulfilling his dad's wish to pass on the business to his son. The business had been meant for Chaz, but once Will ruined his brother's future, it was his turn to step up. He tried to shake off his melancholy. What was done was done. He was the Dr. Levi in the family now.

After work, drawn by the obnoxious sounds of Jasmine and Tony laughing a ridiculous amount while loud rock music blared, Will went out to see what the big fuss was about. He stood in the doorway of his waiting room, becoming more and more tense while he was not watching Jasmine boogie to Aerosmith's "Walk this Way." She held one ankle and did this weird muscle-flexing thing. She wiggled and waved her body, perfectly matching the dancer on screen. When she did a headstand with Tony holding her ankle that had both of them smiling, Will left.

He decided then and there that if Tony was man enough to dance and take tap classes to meet women, then Will was man enough to join a knitting club to meet women. Clearly, it had worked for Tony.

Maybe Will would meet someone over eighteen, frisky, and fun.

CHAPTER FIVE

Will met lots of women over eighteen, frisky, and fun the next morning at the knitting club in the Clover Park Library's meeting room. Unfortunately, they were also all over sixty. He really should've known better. That was what a sex-deprived brain could do to a guy—make him delusional. Especially with Jasmine around, getting him worked up all the time in both the aggravated and (inconveniently) turned-on kind of way.

He froze in the doorway.

"Hello, honey!" one white-haired woman called. "Are you here for the knitting club? New members are always welcome."

"I, uh, I'm not sure," he said.

"Well, what are you here for, young man?" a woman with pinched lips and a pinched expression asked.

"Never mind." He started to back away, but a firm

hand on his back pushed him back in.

"He's one of us," a voice announced as she dragged him into the room. She wore a leopard print leotard with bright pink pants. Her hair was white and short with spikes on top.

"Maggie!" one of the women exclaimed. "You're back!"

"The next generation of O'Hares have arrived!" Maggie announced. "I've got three great-grandbabies and one on the way." She whipped pictures out of her purse, and the women started passing them around. "The twins are Ryan and Liz's girls, May and Alice; the other cutie is Shane and Rachel's little Abby. Trav and Daisy have one on the way this November. Another boy." She pulled Will in to take a seat around a conference table. "That's a lot of booties, hats, and blankets I've got to knit. You ladies know who this is?" She pointed at Will.

Will startled. She knew him?

"This is Brian's son," Maggie said. "From Levi Orthodontics."

All the women spoke at once about their son, daughter, or grandkid that went to Levi Orthodontics. Then they went back to oohing and aahing over Maggie's great-grandbabies. After they'd tired of asking about the babies and sharing their own grandbabies' pictures, Maggie brought the conversation back to him.

"Remember little Will?" Maggie turned to him. "Or are you Charlie? I seem to remember Charlie was the more serious one."

He smiled tightly. "I'm Will."

A chorus of hellos went around the room. "Hello," Will said. "I'm not sure what I'm doing here. I saw your flyer at Garner's that said 'Relaxation Guaranteed,' and—"

"Knitting is very relaxing," a woman with her hair in a messy bun said. "I'm Pam. And this is Diane." She indicated the pinched-lip woman next to her. "And Shirley, Barbara, and Pat. You met Maggie."

"Nice to meet you." Will fidgeted. He still wasn't sure if he really belonged here. Clearly he wasn't going to meet any women close to his age at the knitting club.

Maggie set some knitting needles and gray yarn in front of him.

"I don't know how to knit," he said. "I'll just go." He started to stand when Maggie yanked him back down. She was surprisingly strong for a woman over sixty. She might even be over seventy.

"Now if there was ever a person in need of relaxation, it's you," Maggie declared. "I haven't seen a man wound so tight in forever." Maggie made a quick loop and started the yarn on the needle for him. "I remember your mom chasing you around town whenever she came to visit your dad at work. You were the wild child. What happened to you?"

His shoulders slumped. "Life happened."

Maggie patted his knee. "First comes knitting; then we'll figure out life."

The women chorused their agreement. Everyone started knitting, and there was nothing but the soft *click-clack* of needles.

"I heard you took over your dad's practice," Maggie said to him. "You like it?"

Did he like it? He considered the question. If he had to have a job, he figured it was as good as any. And it was too late now anyway after seven years of dental school.

"It's satisfying work," he replied in case they had any grandkids they wanted to send his way.

Maggie grunted. Then she gave him a quick lesson on the knit stitch. He got the hang of it on the third try. His fingers were strong and nimble from working with braces and the various tools needed to clamp, tighten, and remove metalwork. A half an hour later, Will was in the groove and approaching a Zen state as the women chattered on around him. This *was* relaxing. The busyness of his fingers; the single focus on accomplishing one thing that produced results right in front of his eyes. The soft voices.

Time passed quickly when he suddenly realized the women were packing up.

"You got a woman, Will?" Maggie asked.

The other women looked at him expectantly. If he said no, they'd whip out pictures of their eligible granddaughters.

"Yes," he said. He did have an anonymous over eighteen, fun, and frisky female he corresponded with every night. He still hadn't met her, but from their conversations it seemed like they got along well enough to soon move to an in-person conversation.

Maggie looked at him suspiciously. "Then why are you so tense? You need a little bedroom advice?"

"How to kick it up a notch?" Pam asked sweetly.

"You stole that from Emeril!" Diane accused.

"Well, I didn't want to be crass," Pam said. "Would you like me to say score a home run?"

"Hide the salami," Shirley put in.

"Do the wild thing," Barbara caroled.

Will stood and held up a hand, but not before Pat declared, "The fill and drill!"

Will's ears burned. Maggie turned to Pat. "He's an orthodontist, not a dentist. More like a clamp and release. Right, Will?"

Will cleared his throat. "Thank you for the lesson. Goodbye." He turned to go.

"See you next week, Will," Maggie said. "I want to

see progress on that scarf you're making. And I want those needles back, so you *have* to come back."

For some reason it felt more like a threat than a cheery goodbye. He waved over his shoulder and headed out the door, glad no one he knew was hanging around the library. This would be his little secret. He worked the late shift at the office on Tuesdays, so no one there would ever have to know. He went straight home and knit until it was time for work. He felt more relaxed than he had in a long time. The yarn was so soft too. Something like this, a soft knitted item, was exactly what Jasmine needed to soften her up.

~ ~ ~

Over the weekend Will stopped at a yarn store in Eastman to pick up his own set of knitting needles and some deep forest green yarn for another scarf. While he was poking around in there he found some hand-knitted items for sale. The white fingerless gloves caught his eye. They were super soft. He bought them on impulse, thinking that a soft gift was exactly what Jasmine needed to tenderize her. Of course, he wouldn't just hand it to her. It would be an anonymous gift, and if she gradually softened up, maybe they'd have fewer arguments over noise and parking and that awful tap class that clashed with his evening hours. It really was a horrendous racket coming out of that studio on Tuesday evenings. Now that he was finding some peace at home, between his knitting and his online chatting, he'd like to find some peace at work as well.

Tony didn't make that easy. Monday morning, Will caught sight of Tony walking past his office with a massive black wheel. Will scrambled to his feet. "What is that?"

"Oh, hey, Dr. Will! You're here early. Heh-heh-heh." Had Tony been hoping to sneak by him with this monstrosity?

Tony set down the giant wheel and turned it to face him. "It's a prize wheel. To reward kids who avoid all the stuff that doesn't get along with braces. You know—chewy candies, soda, sugar, gum—"

"I know! This isn't *Wheel of Fortune*! It's bad enough we've got a video game system. I can barely get the patients out of the waiting room and into the chair for their appointment."

Tony spun the wheel. "Look, free pizza slice." He spun it again. "Ooh, five-dollar gift card. That's a good one." There was also free spin, Shane's Scoops ice cream, free movie ticket, free T-shirt, and Treasure Chest, whatever the hell that was.

Will's blood pressure elevated, and he thought longingly of his knitting stashed safely at home.

"Tony, you must clear things with me before..." He trailed off as Tony was already setting up the prize wheel in the waiting room.

Hillary and some of his orthodontic assistants, Jennifer and Amy, came out to see. "Ooh, this is fun," Hillary said. Jennifer and Amy agreed.

Will sighed, outnumbered in his own office. "I'm not administering prizes or spinning the wheel."

"No prob," Tony said. "The patients spin the wheel. Hillary here has all the prizes. I already bought a month's supply!"

Will's lips formed a flat line. Going to the orthodontist wasn't a carnival ride. It was a professional appointment geared to healthy beautiful smiles. He was about to say so when Tony dropped another bombshell.

"I'm taking us online too," Tony said. "Hillary is helping me set up a massive social media campaign. We want to reach our patients where they live."

"Tony," he ground out. "May I speak with you privately in my office?" Will didn't wait for a response, merely walked back to his office and waited. Tony appeared. "I don't want you wasting our resources on social media. It takes time away from our patients."

"No, it gives time to our patients. They'll have greater compliance if they're hooked in with our program. Just think, if they're following our protocols for keeping their teeth cavity-free and their braces safe from damage, they'll have a greater success rate. Faster too. And less emergency repair appointments for us."

Will considered this. It was true that they often got off-hour calls to repair braces damaged by popcorn or a tangle of gum, even though he explained the hazards and sent each patient home with a tri-fold brochure that spelled out what they should avoid.

"Okay," Will finally said, "but—"

"Awesome!" Tony exclaimed, raising his hand for a high five. Will left him hanging.

"But the social media stuff is strictly after hours," Will said. "Only if you have time. And not something required of our staff."

"No problem. It's super easy. You're gonna love the results."

Will wasn't so sure of that.

Tony slapped his knee. "I'm gonna grab some coffee. Want some?"

"Sure." He pulled out his wallet.

"Nah. This one's on me."

Will froze, surprised at the gesture. He tucked his wallet back in his pocket. "Thank you."

Will relaxed a little after Tony left. Tony meant well. It wasn't Will's style, but he should be more open to Tony's input. He snagged the gift box with the fingerless gloves in it, peeked into Jasmine's dance studio and saw her stretching in there. Damn, she was flexible. She was standing with one leg stretched up by her ear. He inconveniently got hard imagining what that kind of flexibility could do to a guy. He quickly turned away, rushing down the hallway toward the back door that led to the stairs to her apartment. He went upstairs and left his anonymous gift by her door.

He went back inside, walking briskly down the hallway just as Jasmine came toward him in the opposite direction. Probably heading for the shared restrooms in the back of the building.

"You're in a hurry," she said. "Braces emergency?"

"Yes," he said and kept going, a small smile on his lips. He was really looking forward to tenderizing her. Hopefully they'd fight a lot less, thereby reducing his stress.

"How's the decibel level?" she called in her mocking way. Even now, he could hear the pop music blaring from the dance studio.

"Too high, Jazzy," he responded. At her silence, he glanced over his shoulder and met her narrowed eyes. Even from this distance he could tell the nickname rankled. At least he had that ace in the hole.

She marched toward him. He waited, casually taking in the leotard and tights that were like a second skin on her, leaving nothing to his imagination. Damn, he wanted her way too much.

She stared at his bow tie, glanced at his crotch, and met his eyes. "Your numbered parking spaces are ridiculous."

He cocked his head to the side. "How so?"

She gestured wildly. "Because the parents are constantly changing depending on the class. You can't possibly expect them to remember to park in certain numbered spaces. They're in and out once a week."

"It's not that hard to remember," he said.

She stuck her finger in his face. "You crossed the line here, William."

"I actually don't mind the name William," he said calmly.

Her eyes flashed. Why did he find this hellion so appealing? He normally liked sweet, gentle women. Maybe this knitting stuff was making him too gentle if he was turned on by a hellcat. Sort of a reverse gender role here. Time to assert his masculinity.

He brought himself up to his full height and stuck a finger in her face. "Back off!" he barked.

She got in his face, up on tiptoe. "You back off!"

He was so turned on, there was only one logical move. He slowly cupped the back of her head, giving her plenty of time to protest, then wrapped one arm around her waist. Her breathing quickened. She stared at him, eyes wide, blessedly quiet, so he kissed her in a very manly, ungentle way. Hard and demanding, forcing her mouth open as his tongue invaded. Tasting her only made him want more. She melted against him like alginate dental impression material, only much warmer.

The front door opened, and Will took a quick step away from Jasmine as a teenaged boy and his mother walked in. Must be his new patient. He glanced at Jasmine, who just kept staring at him in shock, still blessedly quiet. He couldn't explain his actions, so he merely walked away.

He held the door open to his office, ushering his new patient in without a word. He and Jasmine would never speak of this again, he decided, purposely not looking back at her. There was no reasonable explanation he could conceive of for his actions, other than that they were regrettable in light of their basic incompatibility.

But as he worked on his patients, he couldn't help remembering how their perfect bites had fit together exactly as he'd known they would. That didn't happen often. Usually one person had to adjust to accommodate the other's larger bite or slight crossbite to prevent the teeth from clashing or awkward jaw pain, or worse, sloppy lip action. There had been no sloppiness.

Only the most perfect kiss he'd ever had. This fact was most inconvenient and weighed heavily on his mind.

That night, his fun and frisky over-eighteen female emailed him a dirty joke about how going to the dentist is like oral sex—he puts his tool in your mouth, and when he's done, asks you to spit. He smiled. He had to meet this woman. Someone like this, fun with a good sense of humor, was the kind of woman he should be with. Someone that made his life easier, bringing a lightness to what often felt like his heavy burden. Not an overbearing, confrontational hellcat like Jasmine. He never should've kissed her. That was messed up.

But every time he brought up meeting his anonymous emailer, she went mute. It was so frustrating. He really hoped this whole email thing wasn't a practical joke. Like his brother or Tony yanking his chain. He could never ask Tony because he could never admit he'd been preoccupied with anonymous chatting.

His phone rang, and he checked the ID. "Hey, Charlie. Chaz." His brother liked to be called Chaz now.

"Hey, Will. How's the metal-mouth game?"

Will frowned. Braces weren't just about metal anymore. There were also ceramics, as well as plastic aligners. It was a much bigger orthodontic world than his brother ever knew.

"Fine. How're you?"

"Great! I opened another Rumble Bears franchise. Now there's two of us!"

Rumble Bears was a parent and child music class his brother ran for the under-seven set. The kids and parents sat in a circle while Chaz played silly songs on an acoustic guitar. Sure, music was fun, but it wasn't like playing silly songs was a real career.

"That's great," Will said. "So business is good?"

"Yeah. It's all good, bro."

"You wouldn't happen to be Glamstick, would you?" He winced. Why did he say that?

"What the hell is Glamstick?"

"Never mind."

"Hey, the reason I called was to tell you…Carrie and I eloped in Vegas last weekend."

Will's jaw dropped. His ex-girlfriend was now his sister-in-law? Forever and ever part of the family? It was one thing to know they were a couple, another thing to have her be family. Carrie and Chaz had only been together for nine months! Shit.

"Will, you there?"

"Yeah, I'm here. Congratulations."

"Thanks, bro. Oh, hey, Carrie wants to talk to you."

Great.

"Hey, Will," Carrie said. "It's official. I'm a Levi."

Will grimaced. "Yes. Congratulations."

"Are you happy for us?"

"Of course."

"Good. I'm so glad there's no hard feelings. We'll see you at Thanksgiving, brother-in-law."

"Yup."

She giggled, and then his brother got back on the phone. "I gotta go. Carrie made dinner. She's such a domestic goddess."

"Yeah, okay. Bye." Will exhaled sharply. That was one of the things he'd loved about Carrie. She was soft, sweet, and loved to cook for him. For the first time, he wondered if maybe his brother had gotten the better deal after the accident. How could he think that? Charlie had lost everything.

He went back to his knitting, got into a rhythm, and found his Zen place once more.

~ ~ ~

Jasmine wore her new cashmere fingerless gloves to work on Tuesday afternoon. They were gorgeous, warm, and so soft, and she loved them despite suspecting they were from Will. Why had the man kissed her anyway? He seemed as shaken by the kiss as she was, as though the gesture had surprised him as much as her. Of course, they could've been from Tony, who'd been so sweet and flirty with her at their last couple of tap classes. Tony was a really fun guy. Just because she couldn't imagine ever kissing him didn't mean they couldn't have fun together. It was nothing wrong with him. He was cute, sort of, in a pointy-elvish-face kind of way. Looks weren't everything. It was just that every time she tried to picture those thin, permanently shiny lips on hers, she sort of…cringed. That was stupid. She was being shallow. If he asked her out, she'd say yes and just see what happened. Maybe she could ask him to dry off his lips before he kissed her.

She ran her finger along the back of the cashmere glove. Then she rubbed the soft fabric against her cheek and closed her eyes. She'd never had cashmere anything before. She'd love to just wrap herself in cashmere. She considered stopping by Will's office and just asking if they were from him, but she felt so awkward around him now. Were they fighting? Were they kissing? Did he actually like her, or had he just wanted to shut her up? Despite the kiss that made her knees weak and her lady parts tingle, the man was still aggravating, stick-up-his-ass Will. They were simply incompatible. Did she really want to hook up with someone that would then utter the most ridiculously stiff demands about how she ran her business that would set her off again?

Hopefully it was Tony.

She ran through her afternoon classes, ate a quick dinner at home, and returned to the studio for adult tap. She greeted her students, all women ranging from twenties to fifties, and kept one eye on the door for Tony. He made a dramatic entrance.

"He's here!" Tony proclaimed. "Your Fred Astaire."

Jasmine grinned. "You've got a whole room of Gingers."

He grabbed her by the waist and spun her around. "Hello, Ginger."

She wiggled her fingers, putting the cashmere glove in front of his face. He didn't react. Playing it cool in front of the others. No prob.

"Hey, I really have been watching Fred Astaire," Tony said. "Can you teach me that wing move? You know." Then he proceeded to windmill his arms and attempt to wing his feet out to the side at the same time. He nearly fell over.

She laughed. "That's advanced. I don't think we'll be getting near that for a while. But today I am going to teach you a fun shuffle-step combo."

She started class. Tony kept a running narrative of his success or failure with the steps that had the other women laughing. After class, the women gathered around Tony, teasing and joking with him. Not many men could handle themselves surrounded by women in a dance class. She gave him a lot of credit for that.

"Hey, ladies," he said, taking them all in. "Drinks on me at Garner's."

The women heartily agreed.

"You coming, Jasmine?" Tony asked.

She was torn. If Tony was really interested in her, wouldn't he have asked only her out for a drink? She felt like she was one of his harem. On the other hand, he'd checked in with her to see if she was coming.

"Sure," she said.

"Great!" He grabbed his bag and draped an arm over her shoulders, walking out the door with her.

When they got to the bar, Tony bought pitchers of margaritas for the group. They hung out for a while, everyone talking about the latest town gossip—the rock star Griffin Huntley had performed at this very bar last week. Jasmine already knew all about it. In a strange turn of events, the day after Amber's wedding, Steph had come over and told her that Griffin was her estranged husband. That had been a shocker. She'd helped Dave with meeting Steph here last week (he'd stopped by her studio and begged her to get Steph there because apparently there was some awkwardness now that Steph's husband was in town), but things went south when Dave showed up in a Shrek outfit prepared to serenade Steph with a karaoke jam. Jasmine couldn't bear to watch. She and Amber split before the big karaoke moment. Even worse, the next night Dave and Griffin had returned to Garner's, got drunk, and got into a huge bar fight that ended with the pair in jail.

Jasmine felt kinda bad for Steph, torn between the two men, though clearly Dave was the one to be with. Dave was a nice guy. Griffin was just a gorgeous asshole, as far as she could tell.

A while later as the pitchers ran dry, people started heading out.

"Hey, you want me to walk you home?" Tony asked her as she stood and put on her coat.

Her dance studio was only two blocks away. Clover Park was safe. It wasn't like she was heading down an alley in the city all by her lonesome. But maybe he was thinking he'd like to walk her to the door and pull the classic goodnight-kiss move. He licked his lips and the shininess of that gesture repulsed her, cashmere gloves or no.

"It's a short walk," she said. "Thanks anyway."

He inclined his head. "Until tomorrow."

"Yes. Thanks for the drink."

"My pleasure," he said warmly.

For a moment she was tempted. Here was a nice guy that seemed to be interested in her and gave her gifts. Not only that, he was young, professional, and clearly smart if he'd made it through orthodontic school. Of course, so had Will, except he wasn't nice. More like extremely irritating, aggravating, and…an amazing kisser. Now why was she thinking about Will again?

"Bye," she said with a wave of her cashmere glove. She headed home, looking forward to sending Will another anonymous dirty joke. She'd found a ton of them on the Internet. It was extremely entertaining to mess with him.

She went straight to her laptop and wrote the email she'd been thinking about sending ever since she'd found the joke at dinner. *A stud-muffin dentist*— she giggled, she'd added the stud-muffin part herself— *and a woman hook up. After, she says, you must be a very good dentist, I didn't feel a thing.* She hit send and grinned to herself.

An email dinged back a minute later: *If you hooked up with me, Miss Fun and Frisky, you would most assuredly feel A LOT of things.*

Her heart started pounding. She considered deleting the message as it stared at her, boldly challenging her to step up.

Another email popped up. *Meet me and you'll see.*

CHAPTER SIX

Jasmine shut the laptop. There was no way she could meet Will. The moment he realized it was her behind the anonymous emails, he'd be furious. She knew he would. Her goal had simply been to loosen him up. Obviously that hadn't worked. Even his kiss had been inflexible in a deliciously dominating way.

She took off the cashmere gloves and rubbed them between her fingers, needing something to calm her in light of the disturbing fact that she now had two potential men in her life, and she was very afraid of the way she was leaning.

Her cell rang, startling her. Calm down, she told herself. Will didn't have her number. She checked the ID. It was home.

"Hello," she sang.

"Hey, Jazzy," her younger sister, Zoe, said. "What's shakin', bacon?"

"Not much, girlie, just doing my dance-studio

thing. What's up?" Zoe lived at home to save on rent while she booked regular gigs in nearby New York City as a jazz singer. She was also a part-time waitress at Garner's.

"So who's the guy?"

Jasmine groaned. This was the one thing about small towns she didn't miss. News traveled fast, and everyone's lives were fair game.

Zoe went on. "Lexi told me you were flirty and laughing with some guy, and then he walked you out the door. And p.s. I heard he's fresh meat." Lexi was a waitress at Garner's too.

"Yes, he's new in town. Tony Russo. He's in my adult tap class. It's no big thing. He bought everyone in class drinks."

"But he only walked you out the door. Omigod, is he with you now? Am I interrupting?"

"No! He's a friend."

"You think I'd like him? It's not often fresh meat comes to town."

"Would you stop saying fresh meat? Geez. Go have fun with someone in the city if you don't want the same guys you grew up with."

"Yeah, you're right. It's just not easy to meet a decent guy in a jazz club. They think it's cool to pick up the singer, but not so cool to actually have a relationship. Hey, you still fighting with Will?"

"It never ends. He's so…I don't know. Just so…"

"Aggravating? Uptight? Stick up his ass?" Zoe prompted, using Jasmine's very own words that she'd uttered about Will since the first day they clashed at the summer community theater. Zoe had the lead in the play, so she'd had a front-row seat to the Will and Jasmine smackdown.

"He's all those things." She paused, then said quietly, "He kissed me."

Zoe's squeal of delight nearly took out Jasmine's eardrum. She pulled the phone away from her ear as her sister went nuts. "Omigod, omigod, omigod, I knew it!"

Jasmine put the phone back to her ear. "Knew what?"

"Delilah called it this summer. She said, 'Love/hate same deal.' You're in love. Woo-hoo! Jazzy's in love!"

"It's not the same deal at all," Jasmine replied tightly. Surely she'd know if she was in love. If anything, she was stuck in permanent aggravation. "Anyway, I never hated Will. Hate's a strong word."

"So's love," Zoe fired back.

Zoe was wearing on her very last nerve. "Night, Zoe."

"I call maid of honor!"

Jasmine groaned and hung up. Zoe was two years younger than her and had been in love three times already, which she thought made her more of an expert on the subject of men than Jasmine. Zoe said you knew you were in love when that person was all you could think about, when their kisses made you swoon, and when you always looked forward to seeing them. She only had two of those three symptoms—the first two. She dreaded seeing Will now that he'd kissed her. Had, in fact, gone out of her way to avoid seeing him today. And she didn't think it should count if she involuntarily thought of Will a lot because it was only in the most aggravated way.

She was definitely not in love. She wasn't even in like. She was stuck in an intense dislike combined with an embarrassing, completely irrational attraction. That couldn't possibly be love. If everyone felt like that when they were in love, there wouldn't be so many songs, movies, and books about how great it was. Right?

~ ~ ~

Jasmine avoided Will for an entire week. Or maybe he was avoiding her, because he hadn't stopped by the studio to complain about the noise level, and she hadn't turned the music down at all. And he hadn't said boo about all the cars parked out front, along the side of the driveway, and in back. That was just fine.

She'd stopped sending him dirty jokes and went

back to cute cat pictures. His replies, while not enthusiastic, were still encouraging. "Good one," he'd responded to the cat wearing a hula skirt. "Just need the ukulele."

Tonight she wore her fingerless cashmere gloves as she chatted with Will online and a cherry red soft knitted hat that someone had left on her doorstep earlier today. It had to be Tony. He stopped by her studio on his break every day and frequently invited her back to the office after hours to play the *Party Dance* video game. Will always scowled at her when she did that, muttering, "Don't you dance enough at your dance studio?"

Today, she'd held out her hand in invitation. "Show us your moves, Dr. Levi."

Tony chimed in. "Yeah, Dr. Will. Let's see what you got."

Will had looked at her, looked at Tony, shook his head, and left.

He was still such a stick in the mud. What would it take to melt him down? Make him pliable and reasonable?

She did a quick Google search and pulled up a picture of melting ice cream, emailing it to him, then melting candles, then melting cheese.

I'd much rather see a picture of you, he replied.

She froze. Ah, what the hell. She did a quick search

on an actress people often said she resembled and sent it. The actress wasn't so famous that Will would recognize her.

You're beautiful, he replied.

Thank you.

You already know what I look like. What do the melting pictures mean? Are you melting for me?

She snorted. She'd meant for him to soften, to loosen up, but she could see how it went both ways.

You need to melt, she replied. *Soften up that rigidity.*

I thought women liked rigidity.

She giggled. *You're a stick in the mud I'm trying to pull free.*

I'd be offended, but I'm too busy thinking about you pulling my stick.

One corner of her mouth lifted. She wished he'd show his sense of humor in real life. She loved it.

Just loosen up, she replied.

There was a pause. A few moments later, he replied, *I downloaded that picture. That's an actress who lives in L.A. Who are you, really? I swear if this is Tony, you are fired.*

It's not Tony.

Hillary?

I'm Miss Fun and Frisky.

Another pause. Finally, he replied, *Goodnight, fun and frisky. Love, your stick.*

She stared at the words. Love. Was he falling for

his anonymous emailer? Maybe she should stop. But she was having so much fun. Soon, she promised herself. Before things got out of hand.

~ ~ ~

"I started a Levi Orthodontics channel," Tony said excitedly the next afternoon, stopping Jasmine on her way to open up the studio. He held up his cell phone. "On YouTube. You gotta see. YouTube is very popular with teens. They'll watch us and be begging their parents to take them to our super-cool office."

She looked at him, skeptical. "Yeah?"

"Oh, yeah. Watch."

She watched as he brought up a video called Dr. Foxy Bow Tie. Oh, shit. It had to be Will. Tony pressed play, and she watched a badly edited video of Will taking off his white dental coat, running his hands through his hair, smiling at a patient. The whole thing was set to the rap song, "Foxy Doctor is In." It sounded like Tony rapping. She giggled. Will obviously didn't know he was being filmed, as he never looked at the camera. She could never imagine him performing as a foxy orthodontist.

Tony chuckled too. "Wait, wait, it gets better."

"What are you doing?" Will demanded, suddenly breathing down their necks. Jasmine jumped. Where had he come from? He didn't usually come into work on Tuesdays until noon.

Tony just turned and clapped him on the back. "It's our new YouTube channel. Check it, Dr. Will."

The next scene had Will getting into his BMW. The license plate had been edited to read FOXY-DR as he drove away.

Jasmine giggled.

"Take it down, Tony," Will said through clenched teeth.

"But it's already very popular," Tony protested. "We've got a thousand hits since I put it up last night. Everyone loves Dr. Foxy Bow Tie. This is good marketing. It'll bring us business."

Jasmine turned to Will with a smile. "Yeah, Dr. Foxy Bow Tie, all the girls love when you take off your white coat."

Will glared at her; then he glared at Tony. "This is the last straw, Tony. I can't take any more of this crap. Take it down, or find somewhere else to work."

Tony held up his palms. "All right, all right. Geez." He went back to his office.

"It wouldn't kill you to have a little fun with your image," Jasmine said.

Will's cheeks turned a mottled red. "My image should say professional, not stripper."

She snorted. "Stripper! All you did was take off your coat. You're completely buttoned up with your bow tie." She flicked his bow tie.

He ground his teeth together. "You have no idea how hard I've worked to get where I am today. How many years of studying, hard work, and long hours I've been through. I won't let Tony wreck that with a stupid YouTube video."

"You can work hard and still have fun."

"Easy for a dancer to say," he sneered.

Jasmine saw red. "You think I don't work hard? I've been working my ass off since I was eight years old. You think dance is just bouncing around the dance floor? It takes discipline, strict attention to diet and exercise. I've got the calluses and injuries to prove it. You should see my feet."

Will scowled. "I don't want to see your feet."

She jabbed a finger back toward his office, wanting him gone. "Just go back to your office and tighten up some braces. You're good at that."

"Thank you."

"That wasn't a compliment."

"It was to me."

"Argh! I mean you're wound too tight!" She gestured wildly. "You drive me nuts! Everything has to be just so with you. God forbid someone think outside of that narrow little box you live in!"

He studied her for a long, uncomfortable moment. "Did you like Dr. Foxy?"

She did. A little too much. Will, unaware of the camera, had looked kind of cute. Especially when he smiled. He had this really beautiful smile that took over his face. He never smiled at her. The only reason she liked Dr. Foxy was because he wasn't talking. Once he opened that annoying mouth, all bets were off.

"No!" She whirled and turned for her studio.

"You did." She could hear the smirk in his voice.

She turned to face him. Their gazes locked, and the air crackled with tension. She heated under that gaze. Not good. Will was all wrong for her. They'd kill each other.

"I only liked it for the comedy," she said. "You, foxy? Ha!"

He put his hands on his hips. "You're the one who needs to take a chill pill." She snorted. The words sounded ridiculous coming out of his mouth. "Everything is a big fight with you."

"That's all you, Will. You bring out the fight in me. Do you see me fighting with anyone else?" She gestured all around her. "Hmmm? Do you see me fighting with Tony?"

His lips formed a flat line. "Tony wants you."

She crossed her arms. "Maybe I want him back."

He stared at her for a long moment. She lifted her chin.

"You deserve each other," he muttered before going back to his office.

She marched back to her studio and blasted the music. She did deserve someone like Tony. Someone fun and funny. A man like Tony knew how to have a good time. Who cared if his lips were shiny all the time? Maybe he didn't realize he licked his lips a lot; that could be fixed. Someone like Will would never change.

That night after tap class, Tony asked her to dinner on Saturday night, and she said yes. Because Tony didn't make her crazy. And that was very important in the man you dated.

~ ~ ~

Jasmine continued chatting with Will every night as Glamstick. Not that she wanted to after their fight, but he kept emailing her asking if she was okay because he hadn't heard from her. His emails sounded increasingly worried, so she finally replied two days later that she was okay. Their conversations turned more serious as Will ventured into personal territory, asking her what she was doing, how was her day, what were her favorite things. He was full of questions, but vague in his own answers. He was actually kind of sweet and thoughtful, frequently following up on their previous conversation and trying to get to know her more. He was cagey about revealing any personal information about himself, so she was the same. It was more exciting not to know who you were chatting with, she figured. And Will, of all people, could use some excitement in his life.

~ ~ ~

Saturday was off to a bad start. Jasmine overslept and had to race to the studio to teach her three morning classes with no time for a shower. She was tired and cranky, having missed her relaxing shower and leisurely hot coffee. Not to mention she was already dreading her date tonight. It was the shiny lips. She just felt repulsed every time she thought about the end of the evening when Tony would surely lay one on her. All guys tried for the goodnight kiss. She felt like such a hypocrite. Just last night, she'd had a huge pep talk with Steph, telling her to take control of her life and not let men steal her happiness.

And, here she was, full of dread over a date with a really nice guy. And she was mad at Will too for making her feel like she had to go for it with Tony just to prove she did deserve a fun nice guy.

What was wrong with her? She couldn't think straight when she was around Will.

She took a long, hot shower and gave herself a little pep talk as she threw on some leggings and an oversized bulky, but supersoft sweater. She hadn't gone on a date in a year. That was what all the nerves were about. She liked Tony. They always laughed when they were together. She'd mention his shiny licking habit and see if she could prevent a sloppy, wet kiss that way. Maybe once their lips touched, it would be magic. Or gross. One or the other.

Another bout of nerves ran through her. She needed to keep busy. She'd cook! She set some Italian sausages on the broiler and started a pot of rice. That hardly took any time at all, so she left that cooking and made a rare cleanup of the apartment, sorting the mail, recycling old magazines and newspapers. She even dusted. Suddenly, the smoke detectors went off with a loud screech. Omigod, her lunch.

She raced to the kitchen. The rice was fine. She opened the oven, and a huge cloud of smoke came out. She coughed and grabbed the potholders to take the sausages out. They were blackened and smoking like crazy. She opened the kitchen window. She eyed the smoke detector, jumped and tried to turn it off. She couldn't quite reach it. She grabbed a chair, climbed up, and had just hit off when she heard a pounding on the door.

The smoke detector in the living room was still screeching. Shoot. Had the fire company arrived so soon?

She ran to the door and flung it open. "False alarm," she said. Then she did a double take. "Will! What are you doing here?"

"I'm here to rescue you!" He rushed past her, fire extinguisher in hand (where had that come from?), and ran into the kitchen, looking around wildly for the culprit.

"It was just sausages! I burned them. It's fine."

He stared at the burnt sausages and turned to her, still wild-eyed. "Open more windows. The smoke is bad for you."

She opened the window in the living room and the bedroom. When she got back, he'd silenced the smoke detector in the living room. The fire extinguisher was leaning against her sofa.

"Are you okay?" he asked, running both hands through his hair. It stuck up, wild and thick.

She swallowed hard as she realized that he'd rushed into what he thought was a fire to rescue her.

He actually cared about her.

"Yes," she said over the lump in her throat.

He nodded once and went to the kitchen, where he grabbed the potholders, stuck the broiler pan in the sink, and ran water over it. An angry hiss sounded as the water hit the hot pan, and a little more smoke came up.

"Do you have a fire extinguisher?" he asked.

"I don't know. Maybe if the apartment came with it."

He looked under the kitchen cabinet. A small extinguisher was in a bracket on the side of the cabinet. "There it is. For future reference."

"Thank you," she said.

He looked at her, just kept looking. Finally, he said, "You can't cook."

"Not really," she admitted.

He let out a long breath and turned off the burner for the rice. "Come on. I'll make you lunch."

There was no challenge, no anger behind the invitation. And it suddenly sounded much better than cooking and cleaning her apartment to fend off the nerves over her date with Tony.

"I'd like that," she said.

He flashed a rare smile that had her smiling back. He crossed to her side, held out his hand to her, and she took it, following him out the door.

CHAPTER SEVEN

Jasmine was quiet on the short drive to Will's house. Her mind was still trying to wrap itself around the fact that he'd come to her rescue after all their fighting. She'd thought she was nothing more than an aggravation to him. She glanced over at his profile. His strong jaw with just a hint of stubble, his thick hair that always looked a little disheveled. He looked serious.

"Thanks for coming to my rescue," she said.

He grunted.

"Were you nearby?"

He glanced at her. "I just finished with my morning patients and was heading home when I heard the alarm."

His tone was brusque, and she wondered why in the world he'd invited her over. "What are we having for lunch?"

"Pasta in Bolognese sauce."

"Do you always cook a hot lunch?"

His jaw clenched. What did she say now? "It was going to be my dinner, but I figured it's better shared anyway."

"Oh."

They pulled into the driveway of a modest colonial with beige siding and brown trim. Will led the way and opened the front door for her, holding it and ushering her in. A gray cat with a white chest and white paws met them in the entryway.

"Hello, beautiful," she cooed, bending to stroke its fur.

Will grabbed her arm before she could make contact. "Don't pet him. He'll scratch you for it."

"Don't be silly." She reached again toward the cat, and Will pulled her back.

"Watch." He squatted down and put one finger slowly toward the cat. The cat hissed, baring his teeth.

"He didn't scratch you."

"That was a warning." He extended his finger a little further, almost touching the side of the cat's face, who swiped at him and ran away.

"What's wrong with it?"

Will shrugged. "He's always been like that. He's a rescue."

Will rescued a cat that was all claws and fangs? Her heart melted a little more at that. She had a glimpse of a formal dining room with a glass-topped table and black curved chairs with geometric shapes carved into the metal back. The cool modern look was offset by a fireplace with a white mantel and brick surround as well as modern art with bright colors hanging on the wall. She stopped with him in the gourmet kitchen with a hardwood floor, granite countertops in warm, marbled shades of brown, honey brown cabinets, and stainless steel appliances.

She gaped at him. "Your place is gorgeous! Did you redo the kitchen?" She took in the silver curved pulls on the drawers, the crock holding kitchen utensils, the wood-block knife set. It was so warm and homey. This was stick-up-his-ass Will's kitchen?

"Yeah, I had it done shortly after I moved in."

She ran her hand along the smooth granite. "And you picked everything yourself?" She'd never seen a guy's place that looked so nice. Usually it was all black and white furniture, plain, and stark.

He was busy pulling ingredients out of the refrigerator. "Yup."

She sat on one of the wooden stools at the island. "You have good taste."

He set celery, carrots, and basil on the counter and looked at her. "You sound surprised."

"I love this place!"

One corner of his mouth crooked up in a small

smile. "Good."

"I'm going to check out the living room," she said, peeking out to the room on the other side of the kitchen.

"Go for it."

She crossed to a large living room the length of the house. A wraparound beige sectional sofa faced a fireplace with a flat-screen TV mounted over it. One corner of the room had an upright piano. Across from that was a built-in floor-to-ceiling bookcase. The top shelves were books—he liked thrillers, a shock because she found some of her favorite authors there—but what nearly made her keel over was a large flat shelf with a record player, and next to that a whole shelf of vinyl. She thumbed through his collection, mostly jazz, and a chill ran through her as she suddenly realized everything she'd thought he was, based on his bow-tie appearance and generally combative demeanor, was not at all the total story. This place, this music, even these books were exactly what she would've picked out herself. Who was Will?

She found Etta James and put the album on the record player. Carefully, she set the needle down on her favorite song, "At Last." She closed her eyes and swayed as Etta's voice wrapped around her.

"May I join you?" His voice was husky and close.

She opened her eyes. He was right next to her,

waiting, his gaze through those black-rimmed glasses serious, but somehow warm and tender. She wanted to say *who are you, really?* But the way he was looking at her left her completely speechless.

At her silence, he reached for her hand, lacing his fingers with hers, and wrapped one arm lightly around her waist. "My mother forced me to take dance lessons for my bar mitzvah, so rest assured I won't step on your toes."

He led her in a slow waltz. He moved beautifully with a natural rhythm that revved her body into full arousal. That natural rhythm would translate into the bedroom. She knew it in her bones. If he had danced with her at the wedding, she would've gone home with him, irritating or not.

"Why didn't you dance with me at the wedding?" she asked.

He lifted her arm and turned her in a slow twirl before bringing her back. "I'd rather dance just the two of us."

It was heavenly to dance with someone that could really match her. Their bodies fit, moving together like they'd done this many times before. She was afraid to speak, afraid to ruin the moment. She felt like she'd come home.

"You're awfully quiet," he said.

"I'm stunned."

He smiled. "I told you I had lessons. I can waltz, fox-trot, and do the funky chicken."

She burst out laughing. This was the sense of humor she'd glimpsed in their online chats, but never experienced in real life.

He grinned. "I lied. My fox-trot is pathetic."

"I could teach you."

"I'd like that." His voice, low and husky, set off all kinds of alarm bells in her head. Her body remained in place, waiting for the inevitable as he cupped her cheek, tilted her face up, and pressed his lips on hers gently. Then he changed the angle, his tongue tracing the seam of her lips, and she opened with a sigh. His tongue swept into her mouth as the kiss turned hot, urgent, and she was swept away with it, forgetting she was kissing the most aggravating man on the planet. Because the way he kissed her made her positively swoony. She sank against him as Will set about making her forget everything but his wonderful mouth.

He gasped and jerked away from her.

"What?" she asked, a little disoriented from the sudden lack of swooniness.

He reached down and pulled the cat off his leg, where it was currently clinging to his pants by the claws. He took the cat upstairs and returned to her.

"That cat is nuts," she said.

He pulled up his pants leg and looked at the damage. "At least there's no blood." There were puncture wounds on his muscled calf. She eyed his buttoned-up shirt with the bow tie and had to wonder about the muscles hiding under there.

He dropped his pants leg with a wince.

"Do you want some antiseptic?" she asked.

"Nah. Where were we?" He slipped his arms back around her.

She pulled away. "Will."

"Jaz."

"What are we doing? We don't even like each other."

"I like you when I'm kissing you."

She crossed her arms, annoyed. He didn't say he liked her.

They stared at each other. Finally, Will broke the silence. "You like me when you're kissing me too. Admit it."

"But—"

"Come on. I'm making you lunch." He turned and went back to the kitchen, leaving her no choice but to follow.

She took a seat at the kitchen island and watched as he pulled out a knife and made short work of an onion. His movements so quick and sure looked like a chef's skill.

"Where'd you learn to chop like that?" she asked.

"I took cooking classes."

"Really?"

He pressed a garlic clove on the counter and peeled the shell. "I got tired of frozen dinners and takeout."

She shook her head. "You're full of surprises."

He put the garlic in a press and squeezed. "How so?"

"I don't know. This house, your books, your music, just not what I expected from Mr. Bow Tie Man."

Will cleared his throat loudly. "Dr. Foxy Bow Tie."

"And that." She pointed at him. "When did you get a sense of humor?"

He looked at her, deadpan. "When you stopped trying to kill me."

She snorted. "I just wanted to kick your ass a little."

He smiled, and she smiled back. "Take off your bow tie," she said.

"Why?"

Because it screams uptight orthodontist.

"Because."

He raised a brow. But then he undid it, leaving it hanging around his neck. Better.

"Undo a few buttons on that shirt," she said.

He undid the top two buttons and watched her with a heated gaze. "You're next," he threatened.

"Take off your glasses."

He did. Her stomach flip-flopped. She'd been stupidly blinded by the accessories, because right now with a loose shirt showing just a little bit of chest and that face with its strong jaw and soft eyes, he was actually… breathtaking.

"My turn," he said. "Take off your sweater."

"Will!"

"Wait. I need my glasses to see it." He slid them back on and grinned at her.

"Get cooking, mister."

He smiled, shaking his head, then went to work heating some olive oil in a pan before tossing the onion and garlic in. It smelled heavenly. The ground meat followed soon after as he prepared the sauce. He set the water to boil for the pasta. She felt like she should be doing something, but she was enjoying watching him cook too much to move. No man had ever cooked for her.

A short while later, he joined her at the island, where they ate lunch side by side. She dug in, starving. It was fantastic. She glanced at him. "This is really good."

"Glad you like it."

They ate in companionable silence. It was strange

being with Will without fighting. She felt surprisingly relaxed like she'd had a glass of wine, but all she'd had was water. They finished up, and he snagged her bowl and set it in the sink for her.

He ran the water and turned to her. "I should let Sweetie out of confinement."

"You named that hellcat Sweetie?"

"That's the name he came with."

"Do you actually like Sweetie?"

He hesitated. "I can't stand him, and the feeling's mutual."

She shook her head. "I had no idea you were such a softie."

"I'm not a softie."

The man kept a cat that attacked him. Soft-ee.

"How long have you had Sweetie?" she asked.

He thought for a moment. "Almost ten months."

She gave him a look. That was a long time to keep a pet you couldn't pet.

"No one in their right mind would've taken him," he said defensively. "He would've been put to sleep if I didn't keep him."

And just like that her heart opened to him, which was uncomfortable. She didn't let people in that easily. It was just that he looked and sounded so defensive over what was truly a sweet thing to do.

"Look, Sweetie is a barn cat," she said. "He's wild

like this cat my parents' friends used to have. You couldn't pet him, but he was a great mouser. We could take him to their farm upstate."

He wiggled his fingers. "Sure, the magical place where all pets frolic in a meadow."

"It's real."

"Cat heaven is real?" he asked with an exaggerated expression of wonder.

She rolled her eyes and pulled her cell out of her purse. "Sweetie will love it there. Are you okay with me finding him a new home?"

"Absolutely. Wow. So I'll finally feel safe without my pants."

She sputtered. "Your pants?"

"Every time I use the bathroom Sweetie comes out of nowhere to hunt me. It's terrifying."

She snort-laughed. "I can't believe you kept this cat so long." She dialed Pete and Nancy. Nancy answered. She described Sweetie, and they were cordially invited to come up. "Hold on." She turned to Will. "You got time to go now? It's about a two-hour drive."

"Sure."

Jasmine thanked Nancy and hung up. "Okay, let's go."

Will shuddered. "I'm going to need my heavy-duty gloves. Sweetie hates the carrier."

"Good luck."

Twenty minutes later, Sweetie was in his carrier, Will had two fresh scratches, and they were on their way. The cat caterwauled as soon as the car started moving.

"This is nice," Will said over the caterwauling. "Two hours in the car with a cat serenade. At least I can finally use the bathroom in peace. I owe you that."

"I'll tell all my friends. It's a proud moment."

He chuckled. After a while, Sweetie must've worn himself out, because he went quiet.

"Can I ask you something?" Will asked.

"No."

"Why not?"

"Because you asked. It's annoying. Either say it or don't, but don't ask permission."

"What I was going to say was why are you so confrontational, but I guess I've got my answer."

"I am not confrontational!"

"No, you're not!" His volume matched hers.

"Okay, since we're asking questions, why are you so uptight?"

"Because I need to get laid."

She stared at him, slack-jawed.

He grinned. "Help a guy out."

"Have you been drinking?"

"Haven't had a drink in thirteen years."

"Are you a recovering alcoholic?"

"Nope. Just clean living."

"Hmm…so how long has it been since you got laid?"

He blew out a breath. "Ten months."

She clucked her tongue. "That's nothing. You're fine."

He raised a brow. "How long has it been for you?"

A year. A whole freaking year.

"None of your damned business."

"You need this more than I do." He let out a heavy sigh. "Okay, okay, I'll help you out."

"Why do you have to wear a freaking bow tie to work every day?"

"Because it's memorable. It's part of my professional orthodontist persona—the guy you can trust."

"And what's behind that persona?"

He stared straight ahead. "You don't want to know."

"Uh-uh. You don't get to chicken out now. We've got a long drive ahead, and you're going to talk."

He remained silent.

That made her nervous. "What aren't you telling me?"

"Ask me anything."

"Who are you?"

He flashed a smile. "I'm your next lover."

She shut up. Because she had a feeling he was right.

~ ~ ~

Will pulled up to an actual farm with hills and cows and a red barn. It did look like cat heaven. Today had been strange in a good way. He'd gone to work as usual, resigned to a long, boring Saturday; next thing he knew, he was coming to Jasmine's rescue and spending the day with her. And, it seemed, Jasmine had solved his cat problem.

"Do you want to say goodbye to Sweetie?" Jasmine asked.

Will stared at the carrier by Jasmine's feet, where the cat had begun to meow plaintively. He got choked up. "Goodbye, Sweetie," he managed. "I wish you many happy hunts."

"Oh, Will," Jasmine said.

He glanced at her, surprised to see her eyes shiny with tears. He was the one saying goodbye to a pet. "What?"

She shook her head. "Nothing."

She got out of the car just as a couple approached. They looked like former hippies. The woman's hair was gray and long. The man had long hair in a ponytail. Oh, shit. Ponytail guy was Pete Macauley.

The former late-night talk show host. His dad loved his show. He watched them embrace Jasmine.

"This is Will with Sweetie," Jasmine said, introducing them.

He set down the carrier. "Pleased to meet you," he said, shaking their hands. "My dad loved your show," he said to Pete.

"Thanks. Jasmine's dad was with me on the show. The Davis Trio was just as important to the show as I ever was."

Jasmine smiled proudly. Will nodded. He'd heard them a few times. "We're fans of the band too." Jasmine looked surprised to hear it. He held up the carrier. "Thanks for taking Sweetie."

"Well, let's get him settled right away," Nancy said. "This way."

They followed her to the barn, where Will set down the carrier. He knelt by the opening and looked at Sweetie one last time, who hissed at him in return. He opened the door, and Sweetie took off for the corner, disappearing behind a hay bale. Will felt strangely bereft. His only company had just deserted him. That was pathetic. He stood.

Jasmine put an arm around him. "He'll be happier here, I promise."

He nodded, unable to speak.

"Come on in for some iced tea," Nancy said. "I

want to hear all about what's new with you, Jasmine. I mean, besides this handsome man," she said with a wink to Will.

Will grinned as Jasmine blushed. He'd never seen her blush before.

Will sat with Jasmine, Pete, and Nancy at a round kitchen table, listening as Jasmine told them about her new dance studio. They were full of questions for her. As she answered them, he realized how long she'd been dreaming of the studio, how hard it had been to scrape the money together, how his dad had given her a deal on the first year's lease, but mostly what he heard was her passion for dance and passing that along to the next generation. She was getting new students and adding classes all the time as word of mouth spread. He realized that she'd need more instructors soon, and that there was no way her current location could accommodate that number of people. She should expand to a larger space with ample parking. But he kept his mouth shut because the last thing he wanted was to get into another fight with her over parking spaces. Not when he was enjoying this softer, less combative side of her for the first time.

Then Pete and Nancy peppered him with questions about his work, which he obligingly told them about. He was surprised at how interested they seemed in the latest techniques for correcting teeth.

Nice people.

They left as it was getting dark, around five.

"It sure was nice meeting you, Will," Nancy said.

"Thank you. You too."

"We'll send you pictures of Sweetie," Nancy said.

"Oh, that's not necessary," he said, even though that would be nice.

"I'll send one with his first mouse," Pete said. "He sounds like he'll be a good mouser. Just what we need around here."

"I'll look forward to it." He shook Pete's hand and waited while Jasmine said her goodbyes, all smiles and hugs. It was a new side of her—charming, affectionate, smiling. He wanted more of that.

They drove away. He'd miss Sweetie in some weird way.

"You okay?" Jasmine asked.

"Of course."

"You can always adopt another cat," she said. "A sane one."

"Then who would I battle with?"

"You've always got me."

He glanced at her smiling at him. He wanted her. There was no way around it. "You want to grab some dinner on the way home?"

Her eyes widened. "Shit. Dinner! What time is it? I completely forgot."

"What?"

She started muttering to herself about driving time and getting-ready time.

That's when he remembered too. She had a date with Tony. He'd overheard his staff gossiping about it at work. He played it cool. "Hot date?"

"I'm supposed to have dinner with Tony at seven," Jasmine said. "Shoot. We'll just be getting back by seven. Drive faster! I still have to get ready."

He eased off the accelerator, slowing down subtly. "What's wrong with what you're wearing?"

"Uh, baggy sweater and leggings?"

"I think you look beautiful."

He glanced over. Her hands were gripped tightly in her lap.

"Tell Tony you're not having dinner with him tonight," he said.

"Will."

He pulled out his cell and handed it to her. "There's his number. Call him."

"Why?"

"You said you'd teach me to fox-trot. I've been patiently waiting all day for this."

"W-ii-ll…" She dragged his name out like that would make him give in. She should know better.

"J-aa-z, you know you can't resist the lure of the fox…trot." He gave her a slow smile.

She smiled, shaking her head.

"Do you really want a kiss from Tony's shiny lips?" he asked.

"You noticed that too?"

"I told him to stop licking them, but he said they were always dry."

"Get some chapstick."

"That's what I said."

She pulled out her cell, punching in the number from his cell. He did a quiet victory yell on the inside. Hell yeah.

"Tony, hi, it's Jasmine. I'm going to need to take a rain check for tonight. I'm really sorry for letting you know at the last minute. No, I'm okay. I'm upstate with a family friend. It could take a while. Sure, okay. Thanks. Bye."

"What do you mean a rain check?" Will demanded.

"I cancelled, didn't I?" she snapped.

Will took a deep breath. He didn't want to fight with her again. He wanted her soft, smiling, melting against him like when they'd kissed. It had been a really good kiss. He knew they would fit together perfectly in other ways too. He got hard just thinking about it.

"Why do you hate the name Jazzy?" he asked just to distract her.

"Because it sounds stupid, especially for a dancer. Jazz dance. Jazzy. It was something Zoe called me when she was first learning to talk because she couldn't say her Ss. Don't call me that. Ever."

"You can call me Willie."

She laughed. He smiled, relieved to have smiling Jasmine back. If he could just keep them from going for each other's throats long enough, the two of them together could be very, very good.

CHAPTER EIGHT

Jasmine followed Will into his house for the second time that day, tingling with anticipation. She felt bad for cancelling on Tony, but at the same time relieved. She'd have to let him down easy when she saw him again on Monday at work. She'd felt nothing but nervous about their date ever since she'd agreed to it. She now realized it wasn't because it had been so long between dates, it was because she didn't really like Tony in a boyfriend-girlfriend way.

Will turned on the lights and went to his vinyl collection. "What's good for a fox-trot?"

"Do you have any Duke Ellington?"

"Do I have the Duke?" he scoffed.

"Put on 'Satin Doll,'" she said.

He put the album on the turntable and turned to her, hands up, waiting for her to join him. She took her place facing him. He laced his fingers with hers and put his other hand on her back.

"Okay, it's two steps forward," she said, "then two steps to the left for you. I do the opposite. Everything's slow and elegant."

"Like me," he said with a grin before taking two steps forward, two steps to the side. He didn't step on her toes at all.

Encouraged, she kept going. "Good! Keep going. Slow, slow, quick, quick."

He kept going, and they were in sync.

"I remember this being more difficult twenty years ago," he said. "Of course, I was a shrimp and just getting to touch a girl had me nearly frozen in excitement."

She smiled. "You're doing all right."

"This is easy."

"There's always more you can add in dance. Now when you go forward, bend your knees, longer steps, then come up on your toes when you go to the side."

He did. He was amazing—his posture, his stance, the elegance of the movements. She'd been duped into this lesson. "You told me you were pathetic."

The corner of his mouth lifted in a small smile. "Maybe I just needed the right partner." They kept going—slow, slow, quick, quick. She'd love to get him into her dance class.

"Let's get a little swing in the hips when you move," she said, challenging him to a more advanced move. "Forward is swing hips forward and back, then side to side."

He did, bumping his pelvis into hers when he was supposed to be swinging back to her forward, nearly knocking her over. He grabbed her around the waist and kept her upright, flush against him. The gleam in his eyes made her sure he'd done the move wrong on purpose.

"I like this hip thing," he said silkily before slowly lowering his head. She closed her eyes, giving in to what they both knew they were here for. His kiss was tender, gentle, drawing her in, until she could do nothing but cling to him. He loosened his hold on her to cup her face, kissing her softly on her cheeks, her jawline, down the column of her neck before returning to another slow, deep, hot kiss. The tenderness behind his kiss overwhelmed her with emotion. She needed to move things along, so she nipped his bottom lip. His response was merely to pull back, give her one hot look, then lift her, cradling her in his arms, and carry her upstairs to his bedroom.

She knew, with that romantic, sweet move, she was in trouble.

~ ~ ~

Will realized something about Jasmine as he'd kissed her downstairs, the more tender he was with her, the more tender she was with him. And he liked a tender Jasmine. He set her down, and she immediately began unbuttoning his shirt. He let his hands trail slowly up and down her back, continuing to kiss her soft and tender.

She tore her mouth from his. "Hurry."

He looked her up and down, wanting to tear her clothes off, but at the same time, wanting to break down her defenses to find the tender core he suspected she hid under that prickly shell. He turned her, pressing her back against him, letting her feel how much he wanted her as he nuzzled her neck. She moaned and leaned against him. He ran his hands up and down her sides as he kissed her more, working up to her earlobes, which he licked and gave nibbling kisses. She tried to turn in his arms, but he wouldn't let her, instead shifting her so he could kiss the other side of her neck.

"Will," she groaned.

He ignored her, lifting her wild hair to kiss the back of her neck.

She wiggled her bottom into him, and he bit back a groan. "I'm very flexible," she said.

He froze. She turned in his arms before he could stop her and stretched one leg up, up, up, resting her ankle against his shoulder. She bounced her pelvis against his. He bit back a curse, realizing that this—as in all things Jasmine—was a battle with her. She wanted fast and fierce; he wanted slow and tender. Who would win that erotic battle?

He grabbed her ankle and slid it off his shoulder, back to her side.

"How many positions can you do?" he asked idly.

"All of them," she returned.

He cupped her face. "Guess how many I want out of you?" He brushed his lips over hers. She didn't reply, so he told her, because he wasn't here for a performance. "One—me on top, you underneath."

"Figures," she said.

He whispered close to her ear. "So I can watch you come undone."

She shivered, which pleased him. He kissed her gently, slowly, tasting her. Her hands moved across his suddenly bare chest. He realized she'd managed to get the buttons undone. She pulled away, smiling before leaning down to kiss his chest, her tongue rasping over him. He grabbed her by the hair and kissed her hard and greedy, not liking her taking control of things between them. She returned his kiss passionately, her hand stroking his erection as she moaned in the back of her throat.

"Yes," she said as he yanked off her sweater.

Dammit, he'd lost. This was not going to be slow at all. Her bra was purple satin, her breasts firm and perky. His mouth slammed into hers as he pushed her back, maneuvering her toward his bed. She wrapped her arms around his neck, and he lowered her to the bed. He undid the front clasp of her bra, took her breast into his mouth, suckling, pressing her nipple to the top of his mouth as she moaned a low, keening sound. That moan was too much. He pulled back and yanked off her leggings and tiny panties. He slipped his hand between her thighs and stroked her once, twice. She arched into his hand, opening her legs to him, moaning for more. He slid his fingers inside, felt her hot, squeezing him. He groaned.

She opened her eyes. "Wait 'til you see what I can do to you."

He pulled away and stood. "No, Jaz. What I can do to you." He dropped his jeans and briefs and took off his glasses. He ripped off his shirt and grabbed a condom from the nightstand.

"Will!" she exclaimed.

He rolled on the condom, not at all surprised by her reaction to him shirtless.

"I like you better when you're quiet," he said, kissing her to avoid the questions he knew she'd have. He settled between her legs, thrusting his tongue in her mouth as he thrust inside her. She gasped, and he belatedly realized he should've gone slower to ease her into his size, but then she wrapped her legs around him, her feet pressing into his ass, urging him faster. He slid his hands under her hips, lifting her, deepening the penetration. They both groaned. Ah, fuck, this was good.

She pulled her mouth from his. "Stop, stop. I want to—"

He thrust harder. "No talking."

"Let…" she gasped out "…me."

"No," he ground out. He took her fast and hard and deep.

She cried out suddenly. He glowered down at her. "Don't fake orgasm with me. You'll get there when I put you there."

She blinked. Now he had her where he wanted her, quiet and waiting for him to take the lead. Then she just had to push him again. "Can I just—"

"No," he barked.

She leaned back on her elbows and lifted her hips up, offering herself. He stilled, his gaze caught on her sex, entrancing him. Before he knew what was happening her ankles were on his shoulders, and she'd lifted herself up off him, her body half off the bed, still open to him. He quickly repositioned into a kneeling position, the backs of her thighs resting on his chest, grabbed her hips, and thrust inside again. She gasped, and he moaned because this was even deeper than before. He was not going to last like this. He opened his eyes to find her eyes closed, her head turned away from him. Like she gave him her body, but nothing more. He'd have her looking at him, open to him with more than just her legs. He had to, or he knew she'd never let him in, always go right back to fighting him.

"Jazzy."

Her eyes flew open, and she glared at him. "Don't call me—"

He silenced her with his fingers, stroking her center as he slowly thrust in and out. She whimpered, tossing her head side to side.

"You were saying?" he drawled as he thrust faster, his fingers applying more pressure, pushing her harder.

"Shut up," she muttered even as she flushed with pleasure; her body already tightening around him.

"Look at me," he demanded. She shook her head. He pressed deep inside her, palmed her center, and waited.

She looked at him, but she looked mad that he made her.

"Keep looking," he said as he moved again, stroking her again. "I like seeing you so open, so vulnerable, not at all like fighting Jaz."

She held his gaze, her eyes going from glaring to soft as she got closer to her release.

"Don't fight it," he said. "Don't fight me."

She bit her lip, and he pushed her hard, thrusting

deep, stroking quickly, until she shuddered in a very real orgasm, utterly quiet, milking him with her release. He thrust quickly for his own release. She moaned softly, which only drove him on, until he let go with a shudder, deep inside her. He opened his eyes to find her staring at his bicep. Even so, he didn't let her go. He liked having her like this, taking him in, unable to move.

"What's with the tribal tattoo?" she asked.

He released her with a heavy sigh.

~ ~ ~

Jasmine scrambled up to run her finger along the curving pattern of the shocking tribal tattoo wrapped around Will's shoulder and bicep. She felt full of energy, practically giddy with what had been amazingly good sex. The best sex she'd ever had, actually. She felt like dancing around the room in celebration.

He lay on his back, silent.

"Will?"

He groaned and turned off the light. "I really don't want to talk about it." He softened the words by pulling her into his arms so her head rested on his chest. He kissed her hair. "That was amazing. Are you sore? Did I hurt you?"

"Not at all. I can't believe you have a tribal tattoo."

She ran her hand all over his firm bicep and squeezed. "Do you lift weights?"

"Yes."

"So what's the deal?"

He let out a long sigh. "I will give you all the parking spaces if you drop it."

She lifted her head. In the dim moonlight filtering through the blinds, she could see him frowning. "Hey, no fighting. What's the story behind it?"

He grimaced. "It's a reminder of my stupidity."

She reached over and turned the light back on. He squinted, his eyes closed.

"Tell me," she said softly.

"It's from when I was young and stupid."

She quirked a brow. "You?"

He met her eyes in a pained expression. "Especially me. That tattoo was after one of many drunken, stoned nights in college."

She laughed. "Will Levi, a party animal?"

"It's not funny. I partied hard all the way to putting my own brother in the hospital. I gave him a ride when I was stoned out of my mind. I lost control of the car and hit a tree on his side. He went into a coma."

"Omigod, I'm so sorry." She stroked his stubbled cheek, suddenly sorry she'd brought up such a painful subject. "Did he survive? Your dad said he had two sons. Is he the other one?"

"Yeah, he did. He woke a few days later, but the damage was done. His leg is still messed up; he has to walk with a cane. His career prospects ended. He was like a different person after that."

"And so were you."

He looked surprised she understood that. "Yes."

"Why did his career prospects end?"

"He just didn't care about anything anymore. He dropped out of dental school. Now he's a pothead living in California."

She turned off the light. He pulled her close. She rested her head on his chest again, listening to his heart beat. She felt so relaxed and sleepy. She had a moment of panic where she thought maybe she shouldn't spend the night, but she was so comfortable that she found she couldn't move.

Next thing she knew it was morning, and she woke to an empty bed. Shit. He must've thought last night was a mistake. It probably was, right? They hardly ever got along. It had been too long for both of them and all that tension building between them had to go somewhere before they killed each other.

She scrambled out of bed and pulled on her clothes in a hurry. Will returned from the bathroom, wearing a white towel wrapped around his waist, fresh from the shower. Every cell in her body went on full alert at the sight of his muscular arms and chest, that tribal tattoo that spoke of a different man than the one she sparred with the last several months.

"You're up," he said, sliding his glasses on. "I programmed my number in your cell." He studied her for a moment. "What's wrong?"

"Last night was a mistake," she said before he could.

He frowned.

"We both know it," she added.

He took a step toward her, and she took a step back. He stopped. "Are you afraid of me?"

"No."

"Then say that over here to my face."

Jasmine had never backed down from a challenge. She marched right up to him and looked him in the eye.

"Say it again," he said, almost like a dare.

"Last night—" That was as far as she got before he grabbed her and kissed her hard, not letting her speak. The kiss gentled, and she knew she was lost, melting against him, letting him have his way with her. He pulled back and stroked her cheek.

"Go brush your teeth," he said. She slapped a hand over her mouth, mortified that he'd called out her morning breath. She'd barely recovered from that when he added, "Then I want you to dance while you strip. Nice and slow. Make it like a striptease."

"Wi-ill."

"Ja-az."

She sighed. "Okay, one more time and that's it. You still make me crazy."

"Less talking, more stripping," he said. "Teeth first, though. Oral hygiene is very important."

She threw her hands up in the air and marched into the bathroom.

"Extra toothbrush in the medicine cabinet," he called.

She brushed, flossed, and used his mouthwash. God forbid she lack in the oral hygiene department to an uptight orthodontist. She marched back into the bedroom to find Will sitting on the edge of the made bed, waiting patiently. She needed him back in his bow tie to remind her of everything that bugged her about him because he looked damn good sitting there in all his muscled, tattooed glory.

"Would you like some music?" he asked with a smirk.

Grrr…that smirkiness. She'd show him. She'd ride him like a cowgirl one last time and make his eyes roll back in that smug, smirky head. He could have her body, but she wouldn't be taken in by him. She didn't like the way he pushed her to look at him during sex, nor did she like the way he said he liked her vulnerable. That wasn't who she was. She was strong and tough. She didn't like a man that ordered her around.

"You look like you need some help getting started," he said, standing and dropping the towel.

She stared at his thick, long erection, waiting for her, and licked her lips. It pulsed in response. Holy hell. She throbbed, remembering the way he filled her.

She sauntered over to him, stripping as she went, he didn't get a dance on command, before pushing him back on the bed and straddling him. He lifted her off, rolled to get a condom, and put her back on top. She took him in slowly, hissing out a breath as her body strained to accommodate his size. So fucking good. Just when she thought she'd taken him fully, he lifted his pelvis and went deeper. They both groaned. Then his hands gripped her hips, rocking her in a slow ride that was fast becoming overwhelming.

"Look at me," he demanded.

That's when she remembered her mission—sex her way. She rode him fast, eyes closed, and just when she was teetering on the edge of release, he lifted her off him. Her eyes flew open.

"Are you fantasizing about someone else?" he asked.

"No."

"Then why won't you look at me? Are you afraid

to see you're actually with me?"

"I'm not afraid of you. Geez."

He made her so crazy. She didn't even know why she was still here. She turned and straddled him, taking him in a reverse cowgirl position. There. Now he couldn't ask her to look at him.

His hands cupped her ass. "As much as I love your sweet—"

She rode him hard, not wanting to hear one more word out of his irritating mouth. There was nothing but the sound of their panting, their bodies slapping together. She stroked herself, bringing herself to orgasm as she always did during sex. She shook with her release, quietly letting it roll through her, and he went with her a moment later.

His hand stroked down her back. "If you don't mind me asking—"

"I mind."

She got off him and dressed quickly. She needed to get out of here before they fought again.

Will went on. "How many orgasms have you had with a partner? You know, not self-serve."

She scowled at him and dropped her sweater over her head. Once. Last night. But damn if she was going to admit that to him.

"Not that I mind," he said. "Makes it easy for a guy."

She finished getting dressed. "That was the last time," she said through her teeth.

He lunged for her. She squealed and ran out the door.

"You better run," he called. "Chicken."

She turned right back around and marched up to him.

"Oh. You're back." He didn't look all that surprised. "Want to try it with a partner this time?" He smirked.

She jabbed a finger at him. "This! This is why we are completely incompatible. You're smirky—"

"Smirky?"

"And irritating, and you think you know better than me!"

He put his hands on his hips. "And you're confrontational and afraid to show your softer side."

She lifted her chin so she wouldn't accidentally look at his naked...whatever. "I don't have a softer side. That's you. You're the softie."

"Men aren't soft. Women are." He scowled. "They're supposed to be."

They glared at each other. This was exactly why they shouldn't keep sleeping together. They could never get along.

Will finally spoke up. "We should stop fighting now that we...you know."

"Ya think? Great idea, Will. Except we always fight."

He crossed his arms, and she did not notice those bulging biceps or that crazy sexy tattoo. "You're the one with the temper."

"Me? You—" She stopped and threw her arms in the air. "Forget it! Forget this ever happened."

He clenched his jaw. "It was a onetime thing. I get it."

"Good."

She left before they could get into an argument over it. Or worse, before they did it again.

~ ~ ~

Jasmine went home thoroughly disgruntled. What should've been a nice morning after from what had been the best sex she'd ever had was ruined by Will's smirkiness and disagreeable nature. Who did he think he was? Just because she slept with him one time (well, two times, but she hadn't gone home in between, so it was like one time), didn't mean she'd let him order her around or make her feel bad about her non-soft side. You couldn't make it in the dance world if you were soft. You had to push yourself to your absolute physical limits and then push some more. You had to keep going on auditions, believing in yourself no matter what people said about you. Damn right she was tough. It was the only way she'd survived. Fuck Will. No man could steal her happiness.

She paced her empty apartment, which still smelled like burnt sausages, grabbed her purse and went to her parents' house for the comfort of a home-cooked meal and some family time. Her mom greeted her at the door with a big hug that nearly made her cry.

"Everything okay, sweetheart?" her mom asked, pulling back to look in her eyes.

"Yeah, I'm okay."

Her mom stroked her hair back from her face. "Nancy told me you stopped by with Will and his cat yesterday. That was nice of you to visit."

"Yeah."

"She said the cat already delivered a mouse to their back door."

Jasmine grinned. "I'll bet he was proud."

"Mmm-hmm." Her mom put her arm around her shoulders and walked with her to the living room. "So you and Will are getting along now?"

Yes. No. "It's complicated."

"Oh, really?" Her mom grinned. "That sounds interesting."

"How's my girl?" her dad boomed, heading straight for her. He grabbed her and spun her around. He was six foot and, even at sixty-three, still strong enough to spin all of them around.

She laughed as he set her down. "Good."

"How's Pete doing?" he asked.

"He looked good. Farm life suits him."

"Yeah, he grew up on a farm. Never did like living in the city. You staying for dinner? Mom's making roast chicken and potatoes."

She felt herself relax a little just hearing that. "That sounds really good."

"Come on," her dad said. "Watch the game with me. Cowboys need us both cheering them on." Her dad was originally from Texas and a lifelong Dallas Cowboys fan. She and Zoe used to dance around with blue and white pompoms, pretending they were Dallas Cowboy cheerleaders whenever their dad watched the game.

She settled on the sofa while her dad sat in his big ole recliner. That thing was an eyesore—lumpy and a faded brown. The rest of the furniture was newer and nicer, but he refused to part with his favorite seat in the house.

"Where's Zoe?" she asked.

"Spent the night in the city at a friend's place. She'll be around by dinner."

Jasmine watched the game. Her dad nodded off in his chair. The game had just finished when her dad woke with a start. "What'd I miss? Did we win?"

"They won. Twenty-one to fourteen."

"Hot dog."

She smiled.

He stood and stretched. Then he boomed out. "How's my girl?" as Zoe sailed in with her duffel bag and an oversized purse.

"Dad! I live here," Zoe said with an eye roll. "It's not like you didn't just see me less than twenty-four hours ago."

"Don't sass me. Get over here and give me some sugar."

Zoe walked over and gave him a smacking kiss on the cheek.

"How was your gig?" he asked, wrapping an arm around her. "Good turnout?"

"Surprisingly, yes," Zoe said. "And p.s. Jordan is working out great on trumpet." Jordan was the son of the trumpet player in The Davis Trio.

"See? I knew it," her dad said.

"Come up with me while I put this stuff away," Zoe said to her.

Jasmine followed her sister upstairs. She sat on her bed and watched Zoe empty the duffel bag, throwing dirty clothes in the hamper, hanging up a dress that was wrinkled from the bag.

"So…how was your date with the fresh meat?" Zoe asked.

Jasmine had almost forgotten about Tony. Geez. She still needed to talk to him. It felt like so long ago that she'd told Zoe about that.

"I backed out of it," she said.

Zoe flopped down on the bed next to her. "Why? I heard he was cute. And wasn't your last date, like, a year ago?"

Jasmine winced. She didn't want to tell Zoe she'd hooked up with Will. It would never happen again. And she really didn't want to explain why she'd slept with the man formerly known to her as the most irritating, uptight, stick-up-his-ass man on the planet. Because he was still all those things, and she'd slept with him a second time. She dropped her head in her hands. What was wrong with her?

Zoe leaned her head on her shoulder. "Cold feet?"

She lifted her head. "He has shiny lips." It was as good a reason as anything else she'd done in the past twenty-four hours.

Zoe sat up straight. Jasmine glanced at her sister's incredulous expression.

"You mean like"—Zoe lowered her voice—"he wears lip gloss?"

She snorted. "No. Like he licks them a lot, like he's the wolf who wants to put his sloppy kisses all over me before he eats me up."

Zoe did an exaggerated shiver. "That's creepy. Are

you sure? I thought he was an orthodontist?"

She went hot and cold all over at the word "orthodontist." Two orthodontists right next door to her dance studio that she'd have to see for the next year. She'd move after that if she had to. She opened a dance studio to lessen her stress, not make things worse.

"Yeah, he is," Jasmine said glumly.

"What's the matter?" Zoe asked. "You seem down. You can't fool me. Not like Mom and Dad."

"Nothing."

"Jazzy."

She glared at her sister. "Stop calling me that. It was only cute when you were a preschooler."

"Jasmine Eleanor Davis, you'd better tell me or I will…I will—"

"Stop saying Will!"

Zoe turned serious. "Is it Will? Did you bang him?"

"Zoe!"

Zoe warmed to her topic. "I saw you two this summer. All that fighting. There was a lot of heat going back and forth between you."

She threw her hands up. "That heat was aggravation!"

Zoe raised a brow.

Jasmine frowned and crossed her arms. "Fine. I

slept with Will. Happy?"

Zoe clapped and stomped her feet. "Woo-hoo! I called it, I called it. Ooh-ee. I bet it was good. Am I right? Like two flames burning as one."

Jasmine shut her eyes as she felt herself flush. "Just shut up."

"Ooo-hoo-hoo!" Zoe crowed. "I knew it!"

She grabbed her sister's arm. "Shh! Do not tell another living soul about this."

Zoe mimed zipping her lips.

"I mean it. It was a onetime thing." She smoothed her hair back. "Honestly? I'm embarrassed it happened." She glanced at her sister, who looked like she was going to bust from having her lips zipped shut. "Nod if you understand."

Zoe nodded vigorously.

"Did his kisses make you swoony?" Zoe burst out with a big smile. Jasmine sighed. She knew Zoe couldn't keep quiet for long. "I already know you think about him all the time. You never stop talking about him. I'll bet you look forward to seeing him now."

Jasmine's cheeks burned. She clenched her teeth.

"Ooh! I knew it!"

Jasmine stood. "I'll see you downstairs."

Zoe immediately quieted. "Don't go. I'll drop it." She smiled mischievously. "I Will! I Will! Or, should I say, *oh, Will?*" She puckered up.

Jasmine shook her head and left.

After the comfort of dinner with her family, Jasmine went home and settled on the sofa with the laptop. She checked her email and was surprised to have an email from Will to her Glamstick account. She clicked on it and read:

Hey, fun and frisky, it's been great chatting with you, but I need to say goodbye because I met someone. Take care—Will.

Her heart squeezed. After their fight, after she'd told him they were done, he still said goodbye to the person he'd been writing to every night. For her? What was he thinking? He knew they'd just keep on fighting. She didn't want a relationship like that. She wanted one like her parents had—peaceful, loving, happy.

She wrote back: *Why so serious if you just met? Let's keep chatting.*

He replied: *No can do.*

And that was that.

What did he think was going to happen between them? It was driving her crazy, the not knowing his plans. She grabbed her cell and called him. That presumptuous man programmed his number into her cell.

"Hey, Jaz," he said warmly.

She gritted her teeth. "I want a truce."

"All right."

Oh, now he was agreeable. Sure, after months of driving her nuts. Now that he had her all riled up, now he was Mr. A-Okay-With-Everything.

"No more fighting over parking spaces," she said. "I'll take the front. You take the back."

His voice turned husky. "Hey, that sounds pretty good." He was teasing her, and she didn't like it one bit.

"I'll take half of the back and the front," she said in retaliation.

"As long as you leave room for my wide patient load."

"Be serious!"

He chuckled. "I'm sort of relaxed on account of my weekend activities."

Grrr. She took a deep calming breath. She'd called to settle things, not fight some more.

"Will," she gritted out.

"Jaz."

She looked to the ceiling. This man was going to send her to the loony bin.

"What are you wearing?" he asked.

"I have to have the music at a decent volume for my dancers," she said. "Above fifty decibels." Whatever that was.

"All right. I'll put on some music in our waiting

room to drown it out."

"That's it? It's that easy?"

"It's that easy."

She paced her apartment. "What exactly do you think is going to happen between us?"

"What do you think is going to happen between us?"

She stopped pacing and jabbed a hand in the air. "Nothing! You drive me nuts."

"Biggest mistake of my life."

She deflated. "Agreed."

"Yup. Night, Jaz."

"Night."

She hung up, unsure if they'd settled things or not. She hated being so mixed up and all over the place with her emotions. And tomorrow she'd have to deal with Tony too. Ugh!

CHAPTER NINE

When Jasmine left her apartment late the next morning, she nearly tripped over a large box wrapped with a red bow. Shoot. Tony had given her another gift, even after she'd backed out of their date. She opened it. Ooh. It was a hand-knit blanket in a diamond-shaped pattern of vibrant shades of red. She loved it. She ran her hand over the soft fabric. This would be perfect for cuddling under on the sofa. She hung her head. It was going to be so hard to reject Tony. He was so sweet.

She put the blanket inside and went downstairs. She still had a half hour before her first class of three-year-olds. She thought about just walking over to the office and asking for Tony, but she wasn't ready to face Will. She'd warm up in her studio and keep an eye out for him. Tony regularly stopped by to chat. Sometimes they ran into each other in the hallway leading to the shared restrooms in the back. She finished her stretches, taught her class, and even hours later, still no Tony.

Finally, at the end of the day, she stopped by their office and checked in with Hillary. "Did Tony come in today?" she asked.

"He took a personal day," Hillary replied. "He'll be back tomorrow. Would you like to leave a message?"

She shook her head. "That's okay. I'll stop by tomorrow."

She headed back to her studio to do a quick cleanup when Will showed up. "Hey, keep the music down," he said.

There was no music.

"Ha-ha," she said.

"I like this truce of ours." He crossed to her with great purpose, looking like his old self again in a bow tie, buttoned-down shirt, and ironed trousers, which should not have been a turn-on at all, but she kept remembering what was underneath.

She rushed in the opposite direction to get the mop and started mopping the floor with big keep-away-from-me strokes.

He stopped and watched her. "Tony took a personal day. I think you broke his heart."

She stopped mopping, suddenly swamped with guilt. Poor Tony. "Really?" she asked softly.

He grinned. "Nah. I'm joking. He went to pick up a new car."

"Will! I feel bad enough already." She went back to mopping. She could feel his eyes on her. She ignored him, hoping he'd go away.

He didn't. He sat cross-legged on the floor and watched her clean up. She locked up and headed out. He followed her.

"What do you think you're doing?" she asked.

"I'm heading out," he said calmly. "Just like you."

He walked just a pace behind her, which annoyed her. She stopped and faced him. "Nothing's going to happen between us."

He slowly shook his head. "We are completely incompatible."

"We don't even like each other!" she hollered.

"Don't you dare kiss me, Jaz." He was getting all up in her space, pushing her back just by being too close, until her back hit the wall. He leaned his hands against the wall on either side of her hips, boxing her in. "Never again."

"Will," she said weakly. He was so close she could feel the heat of his body through her leotard.

"Don't like it," he taunted before he dipped his head and kissed her so softly, she found herself leaning forward for more. She muttered a curse that had him smiling against her mouth before he kissed her slow and deep, his arms wrapping around her. Her knees went weak, and she felt all swoony again. Dammit.

~ ~ ~

Will followed Jasmine up to her apartment, where she headed straight to the kitchen and helped herself to a tall glass of water. He figured with all her dancing she probably needed to replenish often. She was the only instructor at the studio. He kicked off his shoes.

She set her glass down on the counter with a bang. "I don't even know why you're here."

He raised a brow. "Yeah, you do."

She picked up the glass and drank some more, eyeing him, probably trying to think of the next smokescreen to throw at him. It was so obvious she wanted him, even if she didn't want to. He'd work on that because he wanted her more than he'd ever wanted anyone. Even more now that he'd had her.

She crossed to him in the living room where he stood waiting. "I think we should have some ground rules," she said.

Interesting. "You do?"

"Yes."

"Like what?"

She put her hands on her hips. "Like I don't want you making a big deal about me closing my eyes. I always close my eyes during sex. It's nothing personal."

He nearly laughed. He hadn't realized they were setting down specific ground rules about the bedroom. He thought Jasmine was more loosey-goosey than that.

"Sex is very personal," he said. "I'm naked, you're naked, part of me is inside part of you. That's pretty personal."

She looked to the ceiling and let out a long, slow breath. He took in her long neck that he desperately wanted to lick. He shoved his hands in his pockets because he had a feeling whatever she was about to say was pretty important to her. Little did she know, he'd agree to anything just to sleep with her again.

She met his eyes, and he smiled encouragingly. "Look," she started.

"Mmm-hmm," he said right away so she'd know he was listening very carefully.

She narrowed her eyes. "If you want to be with me, here's the deal. I can close my eyes, and I choose the position. I'm a very physical person. I need to be able to do a lot of different positions and move in a lot of different ways. That's what works for me."

He bit back a smile. That sounded really good, actually. Still, he couldn't resist teasing her a little.

He scratched his head. "So I'm just supposed to let you Kama Sutra my ass while you close your eyes and pleasure yourself? Sounds like I'm a warm dildo." He tilted his head to the side. "You see how that objectifies me?"

Her eyes flashed. "Forget it! I don't even know why I try to talk to you!"

"Don't get all Jasmine on me." He untied his bow tie and unbuttoned the top buttons of his shirt. He didn't miss her watching that. "I think some negotiations are in order."

"Like what?" she huffed.

He undid the cuffs of the shirt. She watched that too. "Yes to your requests, except only I pleasure you."

She jabbed a hand in the air. "Fine!"

"Fine. And I've got one final addendum. Be right back." He headed for her bedroom and rifled through her dresser drawers, looking for a silk scarf. All women seemed to have them.

"What are you doing?" she asked from the doorway. "You're messing up my stuff!"

Ah. Found it. He pulled out a purple silk scarf and rolled it. "C'mere."

She looked suspicious. "Why?"

"For the addendum." He held up the scarf. "So you can close your eyes, and I don't have to take it personally since I'm the one that put it on you." He let out an exasperated breath for her benefit. "This is more than fair. Don't tell me Kama Sutra woman is afraid to be blindfolded."

She crossed to his side immediately. It was almost

too easy. He tied the blindfold around her head and waved a hand in front of her face. "Can you see me?"

"No," she said softly.

That soft voice hit him like a sucker punch, making him want to earn the trust that voice asked for in its vulnerability. It occurred to him that the more intensely she felt something, the quieter she got. Like when she came yesterday and the day before. He throbbed, remembering it. He planned on making her very quiet for as long as possible.

"Good," he crooned in her ear. "Let's get you comfortable." He peeled off the leotard with her help—her dance clothes were like a second skin—and rolled down the tights. She stood there in just a simple bra and panties, blindfolded, and he'd never been so turned on. He stripped her naked, then he took her hand and made her do a slow twirl so he could admire her. Even with the blindfold, her balance was perfect, and she moved with the twirl effortlessly.

He guided her to the bed and pushed her onto her back with her legs dangling over the side.

"Are you naked too?" she asked. "Condoms are in the nightstand."

"Yes, and I brought one. Two, actually."

"Presumptuous."

"Prepared," he returned.

She reached for him, felt his shirt. "You're a liar.

You're still dressed."

He pushed her back down. Then without a word, he went to his knees and pressed his mouth to her sex in a soft kiss. She jolted with a hissed breath, but was otherwise blessedly quiet. He kept her that way for a very long time. He basically blew her mind if her full-body shudders and frantic reaching for him were any indication. He let her grab his shoulders, but didn't move when she pulled at him. She moaned softly with her release. He loved that fiery Jasmine went quiet with intensity. It was a telling sign of what lay underneath, a sensitivity that overwhelmed. Her grip on his shoulders loosened, and she let out a soft sigh of satisfaction.

She propped up on her elbows and gave him a goofy smile. "My turn."

He quickly shed his clothes. And then she proceeded to blow his mind with positions he never would've attempted, ruining him for sex with any other woman. She bridged, she scissored, she lotused, she did something like a frog, and then some weird hanging off the bed headstand. Honestly, he was just along for the ride. He didn't even care about the blindfold anymore. All of his energy went into letting her lead, instead of throwing her on her back and driving into her like he desperately wanted. When he felt like he couldn't take the slow headstand thing anymore, he took control, making her stand to stop all the blood that must be rushing to her head, and taking her against the wall. He stroked her center, felt her stiffen as she did on the edge of release, and he just let go, vaguely aware that she was moaning softly along with his long, low groan.

~ ~ ~

Later, Jasmine sat across the kitchen table from Will with a simple spaghetti dinner that she'd cooked. His shirt was buttoned up again, his bow tie hanging loosely around his neck.

She stared at him. "So, this is…"

"Nice," he said.

"Weird."

He set down his fork. "How so?"

She shook her head. "Never mind." She took a long drink of wine.

He picked up his fork again and scooped up some spaghetti. "I think we negotiated the rules to both our benefit. In fact, I think should any further conflict come up, we should handle it in just the same way."

She went quiet. She didn't know quite what to do with him. He drove her nuts, but then, at other times, he was kind of almost…cool. They went back to eating.

"We had a banner day today at work," he said

between bites of spaghetti. "Three clients got their braces off."

Or not cool. One or the other.

She nodded. "Very nice."

"It is. Tony put it on YouTube."

At the mention of Tony, she winced, remembering she still had to talk to him and also tell him to stop giving her gifts.

"What's wrong?" Will asked.

"I still have to talk to Tony. He thinks we're going out again." She took another long drink of wine.

One corner of his mouth lifted. "Tell him you're fucking his boss."

She choked on her wine. "Yeah. I'll be sure to tell him that."

"I'll tell him."

"No! Don't tell anyone." She jabbed her fork in her spaghetti and twirled it round and round.

"Why not?" he asked in a hostile tone.

Because I don't know how long this is going to last. Because I don't know why I keep sleeping with you. Because I complained about how awful you were for months and now I can't get enough of you.

"Just don't," she said quietly. She glanced up at him. "Okay?"

"Jaz," he said like *come on, woman.*

"Will," she responded like *back off, man.*

They finished their meal in silence. She stood and

cleared the dishes, setting them in the sink. "You should go home," she called over her shoulder.

He wrapped his arms around her from behind. His voice was a rumbled promise in her ear. "I should."

She turned, unable to help herself, and they slammed together as they reached for each other at the same time, mouths fusing together, hands ripping clothes off frantically. And as she balanced on the edge of the counter while he took her with her eyes closed, she had only one thought, she was losing this battle. She couldn't stop wanting him.

Much later, they collapsed in her bed.

"You should go home," she said half-heartedly.

He pulled her close, spooning her from behind. "Shh…go to sleep."

Unable to fight the warmth of his body, the tenderness in his voice, she relaxed in his arms. But she couldn't sleep. She wasn't used to having a man spend the night. Her previous hookups always left after. She heard his breathing deepen. She waited long moments in the dark, eyes wide open, before she couldn't help but ask him the question that was stuck in her head.

"Will?" she said softly. "Are you awake?"

He groaned. "No."

"What are we doing?" she asked.

"We're sleeping," he mumbled.

She turned in his arms, and he pulled her close so

her head was against his chest. She heard the steady thump of his heartbeat and snuggled in closer. "I mean, what are we doing in this relation—I mean, I don't know if you'd call it a relationship. We've only hooked up a few times. But, I mean, we fight so much and that can't be healthy for a couple. I mean, I wouldn't call you my boyfriend at this point, but it's still…You have to admit, it's kind of…I don't know, weird. It's like we're two different people. Like the two people who like each other when we're kissing and other stuff, and then two completely different people who don't like each other and fight a lot when we're not kissing. I mean, what are we doing? I guess that's what I'm trying to say. What exactly are we doing when we're like that? It sounds crazy now that I say it out loud. Are we crazy?"

Silence.

"Will?" She pulled back to look at his face. His eyes were closed, and his jaw was slack. He was sleeping. She sighed and snuggled close again, listening to his heartbeat. She fell asleep in what felt very much like a loving embrace.

~ ~ ~

The next morning, Will left to grab some clothes from home before work, and Jasmine set off for Levi Orthodontics to have that talk with Tony. She knew

Will took the later shift on Tuesdays, which made it much easier.

"Is Tony here?" she asked Hillary, who was wearing a witch's hat. It was Halloween.

"He sure is," Hillary said with a grin. "And his first patient isn't for another hour."

"Okay, thanks."

Hillary gestured for her to go on back. Jasmine took a deep breath and walked back to the open room where four dentists' chairs were set at the edges of the room around a center circular station that held supplies.

"Tony?" she called.

He stepped out of an office, wearing a red and white striped clown costume complete with curly rainbow hair and a red clown nose. "Hey! Ready for another round of *Party Dance*? I've got an hour. We had a cancellation this morning."

Ignore the outfit. "No, actually, I wanted to talk to you."

He waggled his brows. "Sounds serious. Come on in."

She stepped into his small office, which barely had enough room for a desk and a couple of chairs. She took the chair across from him and glanced at several diplomas framed and hanging on the wall. She tucked her ice-cold fingers under her legs.

"What's up?" he asked, licking his lips.

"I, um, met someone."

"Oh." He pulled off the red rubber nose and stared at his desk.

"And, so, I'm not going to take you up on that rain check. Sorry."

He met her eyes. "Wow. That was fast. I mean, I just asked you out last week. So between Saturday and Tuesday you met someone?"

She really didn't want to tell him it was Will. They worked together. It was embarrassing that she kept hooking up with him. She didn't know why she couldn't seem to resist him.

"I really am sorry," she said.

He flashed a quick smile. "Hey, no problem. The heart wants what it wants, right?"

She stood. "Thank you for the blanket. It's beautiful. And the gloves and hat. If you want them back, I understand."

"What blanket?"

"The hand-knit red one with…" She trailed off at his confused expression. If Tony hadn't given her those gifts, it had to have been Will. She couldn't think of any other guys she'd been in contact with lately. Unless a woman gave them to her. Maybe one of her students? She felt a little queasy, not knowing.

"I don't know anything about knitting," Tony

said. He lowered his voice and looked side to side like he wanted to make sure they were alone before confiding, "Just between you and me, rumor around here is that Will's been going to a knitting club Tuesday mornings at the library. Our assistant, Amy, saw him in there when she returned a book. She said he looked like he knew what he was doing too."

She stood there for a minute in shock. Will knit? He made her those gorgeous things? He gave them to her even while they were at each other's throats?

"Thank you, bye." She rushed out of his office.

"No prob," Tony called.

She went straight to her apartment, piled the knitted gifts into a bag, and headed to the Clover Park Library to confront Will because she was pretty damn sure he'd been playing her all along just to get her into bed.

~ ~ ~

Will sat at knitting club, happily knitting a dark green scarf for himself in a pattern of knits and purls that was new to him, but no less relaxing in its Zen repetitiveness. The soft, companionable voices of the older women wrapped around him. They occasionally asked him a question, drawing him into the conversation, but mostly he just knit and was happy to do so. The ladies were in various Halloween costumes—Maggie wore cat ears along with a skin-tight cat bodysuit (completely age-inappropriate), Pam wore devil horns and a pointed tail, Diane a halo with a white shirt, and Shirley, Barbara, and Pat wore orange Halloween sweaters they'd knitted themselves.

He thought Pam's and Diane's costumes should've been reversed. Pam was the sweet angelic one; Diane was sour and combative. He had a quick descriptor for every woman in the knitting club because, in the beginning, it made it easier for him to remember everyone's names. There was sweet Pam, sour Diane, crazy Maggie, clever Shirley, bubbly Barbara, and plain-speaking Pat. It was strange to have a group of senior-citizen women as his friends, but there it was. They'd taken him in, and he was thankful for it.

He got the strange sensation someone was staring at him. He looked up to find Jasmine standing in the doorway, eyes wide. Caught! His ears and cheeks burned. Knitting club was his little secret.

She walked in. "Hi, everyone."

"Jasmine Davis, how are you, honey?" Pam asked.

"How's your new dance studio?" Maggie asked.

The women peppered her with questions, which gave him a brief reprieve. She'd grown up in Clover Park and seemed to know everyone. She began unpacking a bag right in front of him as she responded cordially to the older women. The fingerless gloves, the hat, the blanket.

When there was a pause in the friendly conversation, she turned to him. "Did you knit these, Will?" she asked in an accusing voice.

"What a gorgeous blanket!" Maggie exclaimed. The women oohed and aaahed over it.

"I'm still on scarves," he said. "I could never do something that advanced."

She looked confused, but then she rallied. "Are these from you?"

All eyes were on him. "Yes."

"Why?"

He was quiet. He didn't want to get into it with her in front of all these women. He'd given her the gifts to soften her up. He knew she wouldn't want to hear that.

"Why?" she demanded.

"Don't look a gift in the mouth," sour Diane said. "That's rude."

"It's a gift donkey," sweet Pam corrected.

"Gift ass," crazy Maggie said.

The women argued over the proper terminology while Jasmine stood there, staring him down.

"Maybe we should talk outside," he said.

She turned on her heel and walked out. He followed her out the door, all the way outside, where she stood on the sidewalk, waiting. She might as well have been tapping her foot impatiently with the look she was giving him. She was all huffy and gunning for a fight. He didn't see any reason they should fight over gifts. There were much better ways to direct her energy, as he well knew.

"You gave me the gloves and hat when we were fighting like cats and dogs," she said. "Why would you do that?"

"I gave you the blanket after we hooked up," he pointed out.

"Shh…" She looked all around, guilty-like. No one was within earshot of them. "What does it mean?"

He shrugged, trying to play it off. "I wanted you to keep warm this winter."

Her eyes flashed. She knew him that well. Knew when he was bullshitting. "Forget it!" she exclaimed. "Never mind."

She turned to go, and he grabbed her arm.

"I wanted to soften you up, okay?" he said. "I thought if you had soft things to cuddle up with, you'd soften on the inside too. I was sick of fighting with you."

Her chin jutted out. "So you wanted to change me."

"Don't pretend like you didn't want to change me too. You hate my bow tie, you always say how uptight I am." He narrowed his eyes. "I know you were

Glamstick."

Her jaw dropped. Yeah, he got her good on that one.

"Wha-what?" she stuttered. "You knew?"

"Yes. So why don't you explain why you were anonymously sending me dirty jokes and funny cat pictures while we were at each other's throats, hmm?" He leaned closer. "Trying to change me?"

She gaped at him and shut her mouth with a snap. "How did you know? Why did you keep emailing me?"

"I heard them gossiping at the office after Tony asked you out last week. Hillary said you asked for his email. It's not that hard to figure my email from his."

Her brows scrunched down. "You knew Tony asked me out? Is that why you stopped by my place on Saturday?"

"Yes and no. I knew he asked you, but I stopped by your place because you nearly burned it down trying to cook sausages."

She crossed her arms. "Stop trying to change me."

"Stop trying to change me," he said. "Now we're even."

Her lips flattened, and he could just tell she was working up to a good mad again. That didn't stop him from telling her the hard truth. "You talk a good game—"

"Damn right," she said.

"But you're a crunchy shell with a tender, soft center. Admit it."

"What am I? An M&M?" She jabbed a hand in the air. "You played me! Emailing me, knowing it was me, sending me anonymous gifts. This was all some elaborate plan to get me into bed."

"I was tolerating you."

"Tolerating!" she hollered.

"Waiting you out," he amended.

"We're done! You hear me!" She turned on her heel and marched away.

"The whole town heard you!" he called after her. "Bring an overnight bag tonight. You're sleeping over."

She stopped, marched right back to him, and faced him. He bit back a smile. He loved that every challenge he issued brought her right back to him.

"I am not sleeping over tonight," she said through her teeth.

He took her hand. "Jaz, I really like you."

She went absolutely still. "How long have you liked me?" she asked softly.

He stroked her palm. "Too long."

"Oh." She stared at his feet. "I kinda like you a little bit now too."

The admission was difficult for her, he knew. She

didn't admit to much of anything with him. He cupped her cheek, gave her a soft kiss, and sent her on her way with a friendly turn and a pat on the butt.

"Hope you like steak," he called.

She waved and kept going. He smiled to himself and headed back to knitting.

When he got there, the ladies were full of opinions on his situation with Jasmine. He realized she'd left her gifts on the table and put them into the bag to return to her tonight. He knew she'd come over too. He only had to suggest something in the form of a challenge, and she did it because she couldn't stand not to rise to his challenge. It was one of her finer qualities.

"Ladies, I don't need any advice, please," Will said when they'd wound down. He returned to his seat. He still had a good twenty minutes left to knit.

"You got yourself a live wire," Maggie said.

"I know it."

"She reminds me of the old Will," Maggie said with a nod. "Good match."

The women agreed. He'd known that on some level all along. It was probably why he kept going toe-to-toe with her, instead of just ignoring her jabs like he normally would. Now if he could only get Jasmine on board.

CHAPTER TEN

Later that night, Jasmine curled up behind Will in his bed, loving the heat of his naked body on hers. They'd had a great dinner with steak, roasted potatoes, and asparagus. Will had put out a giant bowl of candy for the trick-or-treaters so they wouldn't be interrupted.

"Will?" she whispered in the dark. "Are you awake?"

"No. You wore me out."

She smiled to herself. One of the things she liked about Will was he was game for anything she wanted to try. She was having a blast riding him in so many very different ways. He didn't blindfold her tonight. She looked at him on her own for a short time. His gaze back was tender and warm. It was so nice to know he liked her.

"Tell me about your brother," she said.

He was silent. Every time she looked at his tattoo, she remembered what he'd said about the accident.

But she wanted to know more. What happened to Charlie after that? Why was Will still so guilty?

"What's he like now?" she asked.

He let out a long breath and turned onto his back. "Why do you save all your words for the dark? I'm half asleep."

"Didn't you ever have a slumber party? That's when all the best conversations happen."

He snorted. "No, I didn't have a slumber party. That's a girl thing."

She didn't comment on the girl thing. He cooked and knitted, which some would say were girl things, but she liked him doing those things, so she kept her mouth shut.

"Is he okay?" she asked.

"He'll never be the same again."

"Is that why you feel so guilty?"

"Yes."

"Can I meet him?"

"He lives in California. Now go to sleep." He pulled her close, so her head was resting on his chest.

She lifted her head. "Will?"

He pushed her head back down. "I'm sleeping."

"I'll tell you one thing if you tell me one thing."

He groaned.

"Anything you want to know. Or we could do truth or dare, and I'll do anything."

A beat passed. "Anything?"

She grinned. "Yes."

"Okay. Charlie makes everyone call him Chaz now. He walks with a damn cane, and he's been adrift ever since the accident, thanks to me."

She heard the bitterness in his voice and rubbed his arm to soothe him.

"Your turn," he said. "It's a dare."

"Not surprised."

"I dare you to tell your family and friends about us."

"That's a big dare."

"Just your family, then. Unless you're…chicken."

She propped up on her elbow to look at him. In the dim moonlight, she could see he was smiling. "I'm not falling for that chicken bit again. All right. I'll tell my family, even though it's completely embarrassing."

"Why is it embarrassing?" he huffed. "I'm a single professional with a nice house. What's so wrong with that?"

She ducked her head back on his chest, not wanting to meet his eyes. "It's embarrassing because I complained about you so much. You know, because of the way we used to fight before you became reasonable."

He pulled her on top of him. "Before *I* became reasonable? Try again."

"If you insist," she said before kissing him. His hands stroked her back, sliding down to her bottom, and she knew they'd try again real soon.

~ ~ ~

Two weeks later, with Will reminding her constantly that she still hadn't fulfilled her dare, Jasmine finally told her family about him. No one was surprised because, while she and Will had been wrapped in a bubble drenched with sex, the rest of the town had been gossiping about them, thanks to the chatty knitting club who'd witnessed their confrontation. She felt ridiculous. Even Will was a little embarrassed to hear that people were calling him Dr. Foxy behind his back ever since that YouTube video Tony had posted. Even worse, her parents told her to invite him for Thanksgiving. She'd been putting off asking him. It just felt like too big a deal. Meeting the family and all that. She'd never brought a guy home for Thanksgiving before. Actually, she'd never brought a guy home period.

She waited until they were in bed, lights out, the week before Thanksgiving to ask him. His back was to her, and his breathing had deepened.

"Will?" she whispered. "You awake?"

He groaned.

"My parents invited you to come over for

Thanksgiving. You don't have to go. I'm required to ask. That's all. Good night."

He rolled to his side and pulled her so they faced each other, slipping his leg between hers, and wrapping his arms around her. "I'll go."

"You will?"

"Yes."

"But what about your family?"

Silence.

"Will?"

"Hmm," he mumbled.

"What about your family? Don't they want to see you for Thanksgiving?"

"We'll stop by my parents' house for dessert," he said before conking out.

The enormity of that turn of events had her wide-awake for the rest of the night. Were they serious about each other? Wasn't that what meeting each other's families meant? Spending a major holiday together? Did Will love her? Did she love him? She remembered how Zoe said you knew you were in love. The symptoms. She did think about him a lot, but that was just because she saw him a lot. Okay, yes, his kisses made her swoon. She did look forward to seeing him. Dammit.

She was in love.

Leave it to her to fall in love with the one man that

drove her crazy. But did Will feel the same way? He was good to her. He cooked her dinner regularly; he was gentle and tender in bed, yet more aggressive when she needed it. He danced with her. He gave her hand-knitted gifts. Of course, he also taunted her and pushed her to soften up. Like he was still trying to change her. Maybe they only loved each other a little.

"I love you a little," she whispered, glad he was asleep. His answer was a soft snore.

~ ~ ~

Thanksgiving day Will showed up at Jasmine's parents' house, wine bottle in one hand, a bouquet of flowers in the other, more than a little nervous. He wanted her family to like him because he was crazy about Jasmine. He generally hit it off with moms, it was the dads he had a rocky history with. They seemed to sense he was a horny dog at heart despite his outward appearance. Probably the way he looked at their daughters. And, with Jasmine, that horniness was off the charts.

Jasmine answered the door in a flowing skirt and a shirt with little flowers on it that tied loosely low in front. Her dark brown hair was loose and wild the way he liked it. He already wanted her. And he'd just had her last night.

"Hi," she said softly, which pulled at his heart

because he knew she was only quiet when she felt something deeply.

"Happy Thanksgiving," he said, giving her a quick kiss. He wouldn't tempt fate with a longer kiss. He still had to pass the dad test. "I brought these." He handed her the bottle of white wine and bouquet of flowers.

"Thank you."

"Hi, Will!" Zoe said. "Nice to see you again." She hugged him.

"You too." He knew Zoe already from the community theater.

"So this is Will," a deep voice boomed. Will straightened his posture and moved forward to greet Mr. and Mrs. Davis.

"Hi, Will, so nice to finally meet you," Mrs. Davis said. She looked very much like she had in her younger acting days, except now her hair was in a short bob, and she had some wrinkles around her eyes. She had Jasmine's height and figure. That was good news for Jasmine, he figured. And him. She'd still look hot even when she was middle-aged. Not that he was hot for Mrs. Davis. Damn, he sucked at these parental meetings.

"Nice to meet you," Mr. Davis said, pumping his hand hard.

"You too," Will said.

"Well, come in," Mrs. Davis said. "Why don't you relax in the living room with Hal while us ladies get a few things ready."

Jasmine mouthed sorry to him, and he followed Mr. Davis to what he was sure would be the third degree. Will sat on the sofa while Mr. Davis took a seat in what looked like a well-worn throne. He was a big man.

"You like football?" Mr. Davis asked.

Will was more of a baseball fan. "Sure. I watch a bit."

"Who do you like?" He gestured to the TV. Will quickly tried to figure out who was playing.

"Cardinals," he said.

"Not a Cowboys fan?" There was an edge to Mr. Davis's voice that meant Will had chosen wrong.

"I don't know," Will said quickly. "They're both pretty good."

Mr. Davis stared at him for a moment. "Care to make a wager?"

"Uh…"

"Twenty bucks says the Cowboys win."

"Okay." Will pulled out his wallet and set a twenty-dollar bill on the coffee table. That money was as good as gone. He could never take Mr. Davis's money. The wager was more in the name of getting along.

Mr. Davis grunted. They watched in silence. Will wasn't sure how long he had to sit there before he could be with Jasmine again. Maybe he should help out in the kitchen. Jasmine was a terrible cook. She could barely boil water. Her mom should know that already.

Will stood. "I'm going to get a drink. Can I get you anything?"

"Sit down," Mr. Davis barked.

Will sat.

"What are your intentions toward my daughter, Will?"

"Honorable, sir."

Mr. Davis grunted. Will squirmed. Dads always knew his true nature. It must be a vibe he gave off unknowingly.

"I know my girl is tough," Mr. Davis said. "But she's also sensitive." He harrumphed. "Gets that from her mother. You have to treat her with kid gloves. Carefully. You get me?"

Will thought back to the way it had taken Jasmine weeks to maintain eye contact when they made love. The way she went quiet when she felt deeply. He'd never treated her with kid gloves. He gave as good as he got from her. Maybe he should—

"I didn't hear you," Mr. Davis barked, leaning forward and pinning Will with a hard stare. "Do you get me?"

Will nodded vigorously. "I get you, sir."

Mr. Davis leaned back, and Will let out a breath of relief. The older man was much larger and looked like he could still throw a good punch with those big beefy hands.

"I'll take a beer," Mr. Davis said. "Please."

Will stood to get it.

"Will?" Mr. Davis said.

He turned, waiting for some ominous threat should Will ever be stupid enough not to treat Jasmine right. "Yes?"

"You're the first boyfriend she's ever brought home," Mr. Davis said.

Will froze. That he hadn't known. He had no idea what to say to that.

"She's sweet on you, all right," Mr. Davis said. "Just remember her tender heart."

"I'll try my best," Will said.

Mr. Davis grunted and went back to the game. Will stepped into the kitchen to find Mrs. Davis stirring a pot over the stove, Zoe snapping green beans, and Jasmine opening a can of olives. Guess they did know about her culinary skills.

"I'm here for a beer for your dad," he said. "And some water, please."

Jasmine grabbed a beer from the fridge and

popped the top. "How're you getting along? I hope you're a Cowboys fan." She filled a glass with water and handed him both.

"We have a wager on the game," he said. "I took the Cardinals."

Zoe hissed. "Ooh. Bad move. You should've stuck by the Cowboys. He's a die-hard fan."

"I figured that out too late," Will said. "At least this way he gets my money and the victory."

"Don't you worry about that," Mrs. Davis said.

"Can I help you ladies?" Will asked. "I can cook."

"Will took cooking classes," Jasmine said with a big grin.

"You did!" Zoe exclaimed. "That's awesome! You can take my place."

"No, no, Will's our guest," Mrs. Davis said. "You just go back to the game and relax."

Jasmine wiggled her fingers at him as he gave her one last, longing look before he reluctantly headed back to the living room for the game he didn't want to watch with the man who made him twitchy with guilty nerves. Because all he could think about was getting Jasmine back in his bed. And he was pretty sure that wasn't the kind of honorable intention Mr. Davis was referring to.

~ ~ ~

Jasmine was surprised at how smoothly dinner went. Her grandparents on her mother's side joined them along with her aunts, uncles, and cousins. Will seemed to be holding his own. He was polite and conversational. Everyone seemed to like him. Her aunt even asked him to look at her younger cousin's teeth, which Will did in a professional manner, offering both his opinion and his card.

Finally, it was getting late, and she turned to him. "Ready to go to your parents' house?"

"Yes," he said with something approaching relief.

Maybe he hadn't been having as good of a time as she'd thought. They said their goodbyes and headed for his car parked in the street. He held the passenger-side door for her, which he never did.

"You've got nice manners all of a sudden," she said when he got in.

"I've got about one more hour left on them; then I have to give up the fight," he said. "It's too much work."

She giggled. "I think my family liked you."

He cupped her cheek and kissed her gently. "I'm glad, but you're the only one I care about."

She bit her lip and looked away. He did that sometimes, saying stuff that made her feel both excited and nervous. She never knew what to say back.

He started the car and pulled into the street. "Your

dad told me you have a tender heart."

"What!" How dare her dad say such a thing about her! Did he think he was helping her? Ridiculous! She did not have a tender heart. She was about to tell Will that when he shocked her with his next statement.

"I already knew."

"I do not have a tender heart! Don't listen to him."

He glanced at her. "You have a tell."

"What are you talking about?"

"You get quiet when you feel deeply. Like when you come."

She stiffened. "Omigod, you did not just say that. That's completely different!"

"This is you." He did a quiet, open-mouthed impression of her coming.

"Shut. Up." She turned and glared out the window.

"I'll show you later in front of the mirror."

"Yeah, keep on dreaming."

"Are we fighting?" he asked sweetly.

She refused to rise to the bait. She was going to make a good impression on his family, not walk in there all worked up and furious at Will. She was friends with Will's dad, Brian, after years of working together at summer theater and looked forward to seeing him again. She'd like to meet his mom and his brother too if he made it out from California.

"Will Charlie be there?" she asked.

"He likes to be called Chaz," Will said flatly. "Yes. He got in last night with his wife."

"Oh. I didn't know he was married. That's good, right?"

Will was quiet.

"It's not good?"

"I should probably tell you," he said slowly. "Chaz married my ex-girlfriend. Recently. It might be a little awkward."

"Your brother married your ex?" she asked incredulously. "How did that happen?"

Will lifted one shoulder up and down. "She liked him better. Said he was more fun."

Her heart squeezed. Until recently, she would've said anyone was more fun than Will, but to lose his girlfriend to his own brother was just wrong. "Oh, Will."

"Hey, water under the bridge. No more than I deserved."

"For what?"

"Look, just drop it," he said with an edge to his voice. "I really don't want to talk about this right now." His jaw clenched, and his knuckles turned white as he gripped the steering wheel.

She let it drop.

~ ~ ~

"Jasmine!" Brian exclaimed, enveloping her in a warm hug. "So good to see you. I missed you this summer. How's things at the studio?"

She smiled at her old friend. "I missed you too. Things are great! Thanks so much for helping me get the space."

"No problem at all." Brian turned and hugged Will. "So glad you could make it."

"Hi." Mrs. Levi extended her hand. "I'm Michelle. So nice to finally meet you."

Jasmine smiled. "You too."

"Will!" Chaz hustled over, using his cane to move as fast as he could. "Good to see you. You know Carrie. Mrs. Levi now."

"Hi, Will," Carrie said, giving him a kiss on the cheek.

"This is Jasmine," Will said. "Jasmine, Chaz and Carrie. Newlyweds." He said *newlyweds* with a bit of a sneer, but she completely understood. His own brother!

Jasmine nodded. "Congratulations."

They gathered around the dining room table where pies—apple, pecan, pumpkin, and mince—were waiting. Mrs. Levi brought out vanilla ice cream and whipped cream, and they started passing around the desserts. She was dying to know the story behind Chaz. Every time she brought up Chaz with Will, he went mute. He never wanted to talk about it, but she knew he was still racked with guilt.

"So what do you do out there in California?" she asked Chaz.

"Just opened my second Rumble Bears franchise," he replied with a smile.

"It's a parent and me music program for kids," Carrie explained. "We're doing very well."

"That's great," Jasmine said. "It's so important to start young with the arts. My dance classes start with three-year-olds."

"Aw. That is so cute. I adore kids." Carrie smiled brightly and looked around the table. "Speaking of." Carrie looked at Chaz, who grinned back at her. "We have an announcement," Carrie sang. "We're pregnant!"

"Already?" Will said. "You just got married a month ago. Is that why you got married so fast?"

The room went quiet.

Will went on. "I mean, you've only been dating since Carrie dumped me less than a year ago." His voice rose. "Hell, Carrie, we dated two whole years and—"

"Will!" Mrs. Levi chided. "That's enough." She turned to Carrie. "Congratulations, honey. We're thrilled."

Jasmine put her hand on Will's tense arm.

Carrie burst into tears. "I told you it was a mistake coming here!" She stood. "I always hated your temper, Will!" Then she rushed from the room.

Jasmine stared at Will. Carrie thought Will had a temper? He was almost impossible to goad into temper. That was one of the things that drove her nuts about him—the madder she got, the calmer and quieter he got. Even when he finally did get mad, it was so easy to put him back in his place. But right now Will's face was red and mottled, and he clearly was in a temper.

"Not cool, man," Chaz said. He left to go after Carrie.

"You owe your brother and Carrie an apology," Mrs. Levi said to Will.

Will threw down his napkin and left.

Jasmine sat there, unsure what to do. Her pie sat in front of her, untouched. She looked at his dad, Brian, who winked at her. "Why don't you go talk to him?"

She slowly stood. "Um…okay."

She left and found Will sitting on the front porch steps, elbows resting on his knees, staring at the front lawn. "Hey," she said.

"Don't tell me I have to apologize," he said.

"I won't." She put an arm around his shoulders. "I know it's hard."

"Family get-togethers are always going to suck from now on. I can't believe he got her pregnant."

"Well, they are married."

"I was supposed to marry her, not him! I was going to propose when we got back from California! Then he stole her right out from under me!"

She took her arm off him and said quietly, "You sound like you're not over her."

He shook his head. "This is the first time I've seen her since we took that trip to California together. We went out to visit Chaz, and I came home alone. So, fine!" He turned his head toward the house. "Stay out in fucking California! Have a great life!"

"Do you want her back?" she asked.

He looked at her for a long moment and cupped her cheek. "No." She breathed a sigh of relief. He dropped his hand. "I just can't believe they got married and pregnant so quickly. I'm still trying to wrap my head around the fact that they're together. I'm just pissed at the way things went down." He stood. "Let's go."

"We just got here. You can't ditch your whole family because you're in a temper."

"Whose side are you on?"

"Yours." She wrapped her arms around him. He held her tight. They stayed like that for a few moments.

"I don't know what I expected," he said. "I'm sorry I brought you into this mess."

"It's okay."

He let go of her and stuffed his hands in his pockets, still looking pissed off.

"I'd be pissed if my sister stole my boyfriend too," she offered.

He snorted. "Yeah. Well, I guess I deserved that too."

"I know you feel guilty about the accident," she said. "But now that I met Chaz, I have to say, he seems happy. He's doing really well. I mean, other than the cane, which doesn't seem to hold him back. Maybe it's time you let go of some of that guilt. How many years do you have to pay for something that happened…I don't even know. How many years ago was it?"

"Thirteen," he ground out.

"That's a long time to pay for one accident."

He put his hands on his hips and glared at her. "You think you know what's best for me? You don't know shit. Nobody knows what it's like to put your own brother in the hospital. Nobody."

"I'm just trying to help you."

He cocked his head to the side. "Well, let me help you! Why don't you stop with all your angry in-your-face posturing and face your real feelings? Instead of being so afraid of your feelings you can only talk to me in the dark when I'm half asleep!" At her shocked silence, he went on. "Or how about how it took you weeks to actually look at me when we're fucking."

"Don't you dare talk about that!" she shouted.

"So now you get to say what we can and can't talk about?" He jabbed a hand in the air. "I'm supposed to open up and let myself bleed while you do whatever the hell you want?"

She put her hands on her hips and faced off with him. "Don't take your anger at your brother out on me!"

"Stop trying to fix me! This is who I am. The guy who did everything wrong and has to pay for it."

She raised her palms, done fighting with him. "You're screwed up, Will. Not me."

He smirked. "That's rich."

That damn smirky look had her hands in fists. She hadn't seen that smirkiness in a month and was not happy to see it back.

"Go to hell," she said softly. "You don't know me at all."

She turned and headed down the sidewalk toward home. She got a block away when she realized Will was following her in his car. She let out a breath. It was cold and dark, and her parents' house, where she'd left her car, was at least a half-hour walk. She got in the car.

"This changes nothing," she said.

"Big surprise," he returned.

He dropped her off at her parents' house. She went straight to her car and drove home because she couldn't face her family and their inevitable questions about Will when she was on the verge of tears.

CHAPTER ELEVEN

Will had royally screwed up with Jasmine, and he knew it. He shouldn't have gotten so mad at her. The timing had been really bad. But the truth was, she didn't get it about him and Chaz. She hadn't seen how Chaz was before the accident. Will had ruined him.

He'd headed back to his parents' house after dropping Jasmine off and apologized to Chaz and Carrie, though just looking at weepy-eyed Carrie had made him an odd combination of guilty and angry. He hung out at his parents' house for as long as he could stand it before he headed home. He called Jasmine, but she wasn't answering. The next day he went to her place.

"I'm sorry," he said as soon as she opened the door.

She gestured for him to come in. She wore the same oversized sweater and leggings she'd worn the first time they'd hooked up, and it made him horny as all hell remembering that night.

"What exactly are you sorry for?" she asked, sitting on the sofa.

He sat next to her and took her hand. "I'm sorry I took my anger out on you."

"Okay," she said.

"Okay? That's it? We're not going to fight?"

She regarded him somberly. "Do you want to fight?"

He jammed a hand in his hair, finding it hard to believe it was that easy with her. "No."

"But—"

He scowled. "I knew there was a but."

"You've got to deal with this thing with your brother. You've got all this anger bottled up inside over it. You're angry at yourself, and some part of you is angry with him. He dropped the ball with dental school, right? You picked it up. Your life took a one-eighty after the accident too. And maybe you're not too happy about that part of it either."

Again she was acting like some kind of damn shrink—analyzing him, acting like she knew better than he did. "You don't know what you're talking about," he said.

Her dark brown eyes were filled with sympathy, which he didn't like one bit. He didn't need anyone feeling sorry for him. He was fine. Chaz was the one who'd suffered.

"It's not that hard to understand," she said quietly.

"Back off, Jaz. You're treading where you don't belong."

"See? You can't even talk about it a little without getting angry. You have to deal with it sooner or later."

His blood pressure elevated. "I'm too angry?"

"Yes."

"And what are you?"

She shook her head. "I'm not angry."

"You act like it!" He wanted her to fight with him. He wasn't the only one who was screwed up. "That's why you fought me so hard. But it was all a big cover-up to keep me at a distance, wasn't it? Only I was too hardheaded to let you get away with it."

She stood. "I'm not fighting with you."

He stood too. "Fight with me!"

"No!" she hollered.

"See? You don't know better. You're just as screwed up as I am."

She pointed toward the door. "Go!"

He crowded her personal space, getting close enough to get them both revved up. "This is how it starts."

She met his eyes. "I'm not playing with you. I don't want you. Not like this."

He studied her, read the truth in her words.

"You're so damn frustrating!"

She crossed her arms. "Just get out. Talk to me when you get your shit together."

He left, thoroughly pissed at her and his brother and the whole damned world. Any progress he'd made getting beneath that hard shell of hers was closed to him again.

~ ~ ~

Jasmine did her best to be polite to Will on Monday when they passed each other in the hallway at work. Her effort was rewarded with a dark scowl from him. She didn't want to fight because now the fighting hurt. Like it or not, she was in love with him. But he wasn't ready for that. He had to get his head on straight and stop living his life in reaction to something that happened years ago. Even his bow tie was part of the act. The Will she knew, in private, was not that uptight, rule-following guy he showed the world. He split himself, and she needed him to be whole so they could be whole together. How could he love her when he didn't love himself?

He stopped by her dance studio that afternoon. She could tell right away by the way he clenched his jaw that he wanted a fight. She took a deep breath. *Do not engage. Let it slide.*

"I'm onto you," he said, crossing to where she

stood.

Easier said than done. The man was excellent at driving her nuts.

"I don't even know what you're talking about," she said in as calm a voice as she could manage.

"You're trying to keep me at a distance. You're deliberately making me mad so you don't have to admit you're crazy about me."

Was she? Or was he the one with the problem?

"Now who's playing shrink?" she fired back.

He stepped closer. He was forever in her space, but she refused to back up even one baby step.

He stared at her mouth. "I'm not afraid to get into it with you because we both know where this is going."

She lifted her chin. "No, we don't."

He met her eyes with a frown. "Dammit, you want me."

"Get over yourself."

He hauled her against his body and kissed her. His mouth claimed hers in the aggressive way she loved, and she sank into it as she always did, her body responding to him even as her brain shouted to pull away. But the attraction was too hard to resist. The kiss went on and on, and she surrendered to it, her hands clutching the back of his shirt, her body throbbing.

He pulled away, but kept his hands on her hips,

keeping her pressed against him. "You're coming over tonight."

"No, I'm not." She'd given in to the kiss, but she didn't want to sleep with him again, not until they worked things out.

He stepped away and jammed both hands in his hair. "Dammit, Jaz. What the hell is going on? Tell me! One minute we're meeting each other's families, and the next minute you don't want to be with me. What are you so afraid of?"

"What are you so afraid of? What happens if you forgive yourself? Huh? Afraid to let yourself be happy?

He frowned. "I don't deserve happiness."

"Well, I do," she said calmly. "And I want that with someone that also believes they deserve happiness."

He held his hands up. "What do you want from me?" he hollered.

She backed away. "Don't ask me what to do. Don't yell at me to tell you. I can't do this anymore."

"So I mean nothing to you," he spat.

She was silent. Because he meant everything, but that wouldn't change anything.

He glared at her. "Damn, I never knew how cold you could be. It's like you really are just a crunchy shell with nothing underneath. No tender center. It's just ice."

"Go to hell, Will!"

"See you there!" He turned to go.

"Don't call me!" she shouted at his back.

"Don't worry!" he hollered over his shoulder.

"And don't show up at my place or here ever again!" she yelled so loudly her throat went hoarse.

He put a hand up in dismissal and left.

She paced around the studio. What was wrong with them? Was it her or him? Or was it the two of them together that was never meant to be more than fights and sex?

Love was never part of the deal, she thought bitterly.

Knowing that hurt so badly she was having trouble catching her breath. And then she burst into tears and could breathe again. She hadn't cried since her grandmother died years ago. Dammit. She kicked her dance bag across the room; then she covered her face with her hands as she cried over the death of her pathetic hope.

~ ~ ~

The next morning, Will dragged his sorry ass to knitting club, needing the comfort of the quiet space in the library, the soft woman voices, the soothing repetitiveness of knitting. He was the first one there. He sat down and pulled out his scarf. Jasmine was back to her defensive, fighting ways. Why did she care so much if he blamed himself for the accident? It certainly wasn't Chaz's fault. And you couldn't blame the ice or the tree. Everyone blamed him because that was the cold hard truth. He was the one that drove when he was stoned. He was forever to blame.

The rest of the group filed in. Soon they were all talking and knitting. He tried to relax, but he was too wound up.

"You're awfully quiet today, Will," sweet Pam said. "Everything okay?"

"Sure," he said.

"How's your girl?" crazy Maggie asked. "Isn't she a firecracker?"

He frowned. "I think she exploded all over me."

"That's not always bad," Maggie said with an eyebrow waggle.

He stared at the table. "It's bad. She doesn't want to see me anymore."

"Sparks were flying between you two," Maggie said. "I'm sure she's not done with you yet."

"You think?" he asked, pathetically hopeful.

"Would we be knitting you this wedding blanket if we weren't sure?" Maggie asked, showing him the pattern to a white cabled blanket with interlocking rings down the center.

He got all choked up and blinked rapidly as he

looked around the room, realizing for the first time they were each knitting with the same white yarn.

"I'm glad you have faith in us," he managed.

"Love always sucks before it gets better," sour Diane said.

All the women agreed. Well, he had that part down. It did suck. And, dammit, he was in love with the one person in the world who made him crazy. He was going to be insane with frustration either way—with her and fighting, or without her and wanting. It was a no-win situation if he'd ever seen one.

He was so tired. He rested his head on the table, completely overwhelmed. A warm hand rubbed his back, and then the women went about knitting a wedding blanket for a wedding that surely would never happen.

~ ~ ~

Will dragged through the rest of the week, avoiding Jasmine. He didn't know how to fix things, and everything he did made things worse. He was working his usual Saturday morning hours when he got a panicked call from his mother. "Your dad had a heart attack. He's in the hospital. They're doing tests—"

"I'll be right there."

He confirmed the hospital with her, cancelled all his patients, and drove like a maniac to his father's side. He couldn't lose him now. He was sixty-five. He'd just retired. He couldn't miss out on enjoying that retirement.

He parked and rushed inside, got his dad's room number, and headed up there. His dad lay in bed, looking pale and tired and old. He had all these tubes and wires—an IV, tubes up his nose, electrodes stuck all over his chest with machines beeping at his side. His eyes were closed, which scared Will, as it made his dad look near death. His mom was already there, holding his dad's hand. Will just stood there in the doorway, frozen.

His mom looked up. "Will, come in."

He crossed to her side and stared down at his dad. "What happened?"

"We went for breakfast at Garner's, and when we got outside, he said he wasn't feeling well, and then he just collapsed on the sidewalk."

"It's good you were with him. What did the doctors say?"

"They're running some tests. We don't know yet."

Just then his dad's eyes opened. "Will," he said weakly. "You're here."

He took his dad's hand, careful to avoid the IV. "I'm here. You're going to be okay."

"Of course I will. I have the strength of ten orthodontists."

Will tried to smile. It was an old joke. "That's right," he choked out.

"How's Jaz?" his dad asked.

"She's fine." He didn't want to get into all the gory details now. He knew his dad had been friendly with her before Will had ever met her.

"I picked her for you," his dad said.

Will's jaw dropped. "What?"

"You should know, in case I die—"

"You're not going to die, Dad."

"I asked you to take my place last summer on purpose. At the theater. I gave her a break on the lease so you'd be next to each other."

"Brian!" his mom exclaimed. "You never told me that."

His dad winked. "Will needed some of her wild, looser side. I knew she'd bring that out in you again."

Will just stared at him, dumbfounded. His dad wanted him to be like his old self? He set them up? Did that mean he was done paying for what he'd done?

The nurse came in just then to take his dad for another test. "Time to go, Mr. Levi," the nurse said. She turned to Will and his mom. "You can wait in the waiting room. Someone will call you when he's settled back in his room." She wheeled his dad out.

Will's mom started crying. He hugged her, trying

not to cry himself. His dad was strong. He'd be okay. He had to be.

She wiped her tears. "I'm going to get some coffee. You want some?"

"Sure."

"I'll meet you in the waiting room."

"I'll go with you," he said.

"I need a few minutes alone. I'll be okay. Go."

Reluctantly, he headed for the waiting room. He got to the dreary room and stopped short; his heart pounding hard. Jasmine was waiting.

~ ~ ~

Jasmine took one look at Will's shocked face and leaped up. "How is he?"

He stared at her. "What are you doing here?"

"Zoe told me your father collapsed outside of Garner's. How is he? Is he going to be okay?"

He took her hand and sank into a hard plastic seat. She sat next to him, waiting anxiously for his answer.

"We don't know," he choked out. "It was a heart attack."

She put her arms around him and pulled his head down to her shoulder. "Shh. It's okay. He'll be okay."

"He's only sixty-five," he mumbled.

"I know, but he's so full of life. This isn't going to keep him down."

Will straightened as his mom walked in, holding two cups of coffee. She handed him one.

"Jasmine, what a nice surprise," Mrs. Levi said. "How are you?"

"I'm fine. I'm sorry to hear about Brian."

"He'll be fine," Mrs. Levi said brusquely. "I'm sure it's nothing."

They sat in silence for several long moments until Mrs. Levi spoke up. "I told him to cut back on the fried food. But no, he wouldn't listen! Had to eat his French fries and salted potato chips. And now look at him!" Her face crumpled.

Will wrapped his arms around his mom. Jasmine felt like crying for both of them. Brian was a great guy, always in good humor, and had been a good friend to her over the years.

Hours later, Will and his mom were allowed back to see Brian.

"Wait here," Will told her.

She waited. A short while later, Will returned. "They said it was a clogged artery. They already put a stent in place, but they want to keep him for a few days to monitor him. Make sure he's all right."

She gave him a watery smile. "That's good news."

He nodded once. "So far. Hopefully he stays okay." He crossed his arms tightly. "My mom's spending the night with him."

He looked at her, just kept looking, and she knew he didn't want to be alone.

"I'll spend the night with you," she said.

His answer was to wrap his arms around her. He held her like that for a long time.

~ ~ ~

Will was surprised and touched that Jasmine was at the hospital for his dad. She followed him back to his house in her car. He was so glad he didn't have to spend the night alone. He knew he'd be up all night, sick with worry, but at least he wouldn't be alone.

He got home, and Jasmine, without any prompting from him, set about making them a late lunch of roast beef sandwiches. She used too much mustard, but he didn't say one word of complaint.

"Did someone call your brother?" she asked.

"I'm sure my mom did."

They finished their lunch, and he set a fire in the fireplace. It was early December and already felt like winter. They sat on the sofa together, staring at the crackling fire. He pulled her close, just content to have her in his arms again. She handed him the remote, letting him pick what they watched. They stayed like that for hours, watching mindless TV, cuddled up together. He was exhausted, the drain of the day pulling at him, but he knew he wouldn't be able to sleep. She turned in his arms and ran her fingers through his hair, soothing him. He couldn't resist kissing her gently. When he pulled away, she was blinking rapidly, her eyes shiny with tears.

"Are you crying?" he asked. He'd never seen her cry. Was she crying over his dad?

She shook her head.

He stroked her cheek. "You know what my dad said? He wanted us to be together. He pulled me into the summer theater to meet you and gave you a deal on the lease to put us next to each other."

She sat up straight. "That devious bastard!"

He laughed. "I know."

"That was a dumb thing to do. I'm going to tell him that tomorrow."

He kissed her again, soft and gentle, and she returned his kiss with a savage ferocity that made him forget his sadness for a moment. Then she grabbed his hand and pulled him upstairs.

~ ~ ~

Jasmine knew only one thing would keep her and Will from spending the whole night weepy and anxious— power sex. She pulled him to his room and ripped his clothes off. He made short work of hers too. Then she was pushing him down on the bed, where she planned to ride him hard and long until he could think of nothing else. She straddled him and stretched one leg out straight, keeping the other bent so she could control the rhythm. Next thing she knew he'd flipped her onto her back, settled between her legs, and started nuzzling her neck.

He propped up on one elbow. "No Kama Sutra moves. You fuck amazing, now you're going to make love."

"This is how I make love." She bucked her hips under him, but he wasn't budging. He was too busy nuzzling her neck. Then he proceeded to kiss her cheeks, her jaw, her throat, her earlobes. Each kiss was gentle and tender, almost reverent, and her eyes welled up. She dug her nails into his back. Not hard, just enough to get his attention. He grabbed her wrists, pinning them in one hand and holding them over her head.

She struggled to get free. She didn't like feeling so vulnerable. She wanted mindless power sex, not tenderness. But he merely held her wrists and continued to kiss her gently. He kissed along her collarbone, then lower to her breasts, placing kisses on the sensitive underside, working his way around and around, until his mouth finally closed over her nipple and sucked hard, making her arch into him. Then he gave the other breast the same loving treatment before returning to kiss her again, still so gentle and tender.

Hot tears stung her eyes as every kiss, every touch, reached around her heart and squeezed.

He pulled back to gaze into her eyes.

"Will," she said softly.

He released her wrists, somehow knowing she'd surrendered. Then he kissed his way reverently down her body all the way to her toes, misshapen from so many years of en pointe ballet. She shifted her foot away. Nobody liked to even look at her toes. He pulled her foot back and kissed her toes. She blinked back tears. *He kissed my toes.*

He kissed his way up her inner thigh until he landed with a soft kiss between her legs and stayed there. She hissed out a breath as he kissed her intimately, tenderly, seeming in no hurry to do anything more than gently nudge her along. She tangled her hand in his hair as the pleasure built, wanting him to hurry up already as she got closer to her peak. But he was having none of that. He tasted and kissed so softly, so gently, until she was ready to scream. She was so close. *Please*, she begged silently, tugging his hair. He ignored her, continuing his gentle torture until she surrendered with a sigh, releasing her grip on his hair and letting him have his way. He rewarded that by applying more pressure with his lips and tongue. She broke with a soft cry, arching against his mouth. He kept going, wringing every last drop of pleasure out of her, until she lay still, completely spent.

She felt his heat as he rose up over her. Then he settled between her legs, and his hand stroked her cheek. "Look at me."

She opened her eyes, meeting his gaze, as he entered her in one quick thrust the way he knew she liked it. She gasped at the sudden filling of her body, the intense stretch, and wrapped her legs around him. He moved slow and sure, and she kept her eyes open, holding his tender gaze, until she felt the tears leak out. She closed her eyes, and he kissed those tears.

She grabbed his ass and squeezed, wanting a hard and fast oblivion, not wanting to feel like her heart was in his hands. His response was to pull nearly all the way out, then slowly thrust back in. He did that over and over, holding her gaze with an intensity that shook her to her very core, and she felt herself climbing again, her body tightening around him, and then he finally took her hard and fast. She panted, racing toward a climax that hit her with a shocking intensity. She moaned softly, overwhelmed, as she clung to him, taking in his last thrusts, still riding the wave of her own climax.

After, she was embarrassed and mad about her tears. "Don't do that again."

He was still on top of her, still inside her. He stroked her hair back. "That's how it's going to be from now on."

"I don't like it." She felt exposed, raw and vulnerable.

"You liked it." He rolled off her and lay on his back.

She sat up to get out of bed, and his hand shot out, gripping her arm, keeping her pinned there. "Stop hiding from me," he said. "You always hide behind a shell."

"I'm not hiding!" She jerked her arm out of his grip. She'd cried in front of him. How was that hiding?

He glared at her. "You're just like me, so don't act like you're better."

"I am not like you," she huffed. "You're the one who's afraid to just be yourself."

"You don't know me at all!" they hollered at the same time.

He smirked. "You're so predictable."

That smirkiness irked her beyond belief. "You think you know me better than I know myself? You don't. Fuck this."

She got out of bed, yanked her clothes on, and stormed out. She was halfway down the stairs when he called her name. She stopped and let out a breath. Then she turned, went back upstairs, and peeked her head in his bedroom.

"What?" she snapped.

"Don't leave me alone tonight," he said quietly.

Her heart just about broke in two with the pain she heard in his voice. He was worried about his dad, and she shouldn't be making things harder for him.

She scooted back in bed, turned off the light, and wrapped her arms around him.

"I'm so tired," he mumbled.

She lay there in the dark, still feeling way too vulnerable, but unable to leave knowing he was in so much pain. She listened as his breathing deepened. A short while later, his arms loosened around her, and he flopped to his back. She cuddled up against his side. Having sex with a lot of emotion behind it was overwhelming for her for a reason. One she'd never told another soul. It had happened so long ago, it shouldn't affect her now, but somehow it did, and it was coming between them. She should tell Will, but she wasn't sure if she could get the words out. About how humiliated she was, how betrayed, how she had a breakdown.

She loved Will. Even though they still fought a lot, she did. She should be able to tell him. The only man she'd ever truly loved.

"Will, are you awake?"

No response. And because it weighed so heavily on her mind and heart, and because he was asleep, she told him everything.

CHAPTER TWELVE

"I've never told anyone this," Jasmine said. "Not a soul," she added in a whisper.

Will lay there in the dark, listening as Jasmine spilled her guts. He'd never heard her so raw, so open, and knew it was only the fact that she thought he was sleeping that allowed her to continue. He was a light sleeper and always woke when she asked him if he was awake, but he'd been too tired to talk, so he'd stayed quiet. Part of him was glad that he did, but part of him was dying to hold her tight and soothe the pain of what she revealed.

"I was a virgin," she confessed. "He knew that. Hell, he probably liked that."

Will already wanted to kill the guy. Some choreographer who'd taken advantage of nineteen-year-old Jasmine, who was thrilled to have the guy's attention and be front and center for the first time in a Broadway show.

She went on. "He was so gentle and tender, like you. When we had sex for the first time, he gazed into my eyes and told me he knew the moment we met was fate. That he loved me and always would." She got so quiet, he barely heard the next words. "I thought I loved him too."

A few moments passed in silence, and he held his breath. "A few weeks later, another dancer in the show hurt her ankle. After she left, a new young dancer took her place. Mark moved in on her next. He not only dumped me, he demoted me to the back of the group. That's really bad in dance. The other dancers were spiteful. They told me I got what I deserved for trying to sleep my way to a better role. Of course, I never thought about it that way. I'd already earned my lead role before we got together, or maybe that was all part of his plan. I don't know. Some of the older dancers knew his reputation, but no one warned me. I—" Her voice broke, and Will's throat got tight.

She sniffled. "I confronted him privately. I told him that just because we broke up didn't mean I should lose my spot. I was just as good a dancer as the new girl. He told me to quit if I didn't like it. That there were hundreds of girls just like me dying to take my place."

She got quiet, and just when he thought he wasn't going to hear the rest of the story, she spoke again.

"The next day at rehearsal, he was horribly critical of me, constantly complaining about my posture, my hip swivel, my toe point, everything. Finally, he made me dance solo in front of everyone. Then he announced in this really slimy voice that I had just shown what *not* to do. I was so humiliated, and then he eyed me up and down, and told everyone that my *performance* was subpar. Everyone was snickering because they all knew he really meant my performance in bed." The next part came out whisper soft. "I wanted to die.

"And then he fired me."

Will clamped his mouth shut over the roar of protest he wanted to make on her behalf.

She went on in a rush. "I couldn't take the betrayal of what I thought was my first love; the way it seemed everyone had turned against me. I holed up in my apartment and stopped eating. For two days. And then, well, thank God for tiny city apartments, right? I had two roommates who noticed. I didn't tell them what happened, but one of them called my mom. She came and got me. I went home for two weeks where she totally babied me and didn't push me to talk, though I know she was dying to know the whole story. I told her it was just a broken heart, but…it felt more like a broken me." Will's chest ached as her voice got softer with the painful memories. "I was such a wreck. I probably would've just stayed home forever."

But she didn't. That wasn't his Jasmine. She was a fighter.

Jasmine continued. "So, at the end of two weeks, my mom said—I remember this so clearly—'Are you giving up your dream, or are you going to fight for it?' Of course, I was a fighter. I couldn't have made it to Broadway at nineteen if I wasn't. She knew that. So I said, 'Let's go.' I headed upstairs to get my suitcase, and she stopped me. She said, 'It's already in the car.'" Jasmine laughed ruefully. "So that's the pathetic truth. I thought I was in love once, had a total breakdown over it, and here I am, barely able to look at anyone during sex because it makes me feel too much, makes me scared and raw. Like my heart's sitting right there in your hands about to be crushed."

She let out a big sigh and got quiet. Several moments later, she appeared to be sleeping. He risked a look down. Yup. Sound asleep. He tightened his arms around her. It killed him to think of Jasmine so distraught that she had a breakdown. He would take such good care of her heart if she ever trusted him with it.

Now he really couldn't sleep. He kept thinking about the different sides of Jasmine—so tough, so angry, and yet so vulnerable. And that one tiny part of him that had been holding back finally gave up the fight as he admitted to himself just how much he loved her. He stroked her hair as she slept, thinking hard. Should he tell her he heard the whole thing? Tell her that he understood and reassure her that she could trust him? She'd probably be furious that he stayed quiet so long while she shared what was so personal, so painful she'd never told another soul.

He finally concluded that the only logical move was to marry her. He loved her and was pretty sure she loved him, though she hadn't said it. She wouldn't feel like her heart was sitting in his hands if she didn't feel a lot for him. He hadn't said the words either, but they were in every kiss, every touch, and her tears told him that she felt his love too.

Marriage would prove to her in the strongest way possible that her love was safe with him and was returned. That settled, he finally fell asleep.

~ ~ ~

Will went back to the hospital the next afternoon as soon as his mom said it was okay to visit. Jasmine had left early this morning, unusually quiet, asking him to call with an update on his dad. He hadn't been sure what to say after her late-night confessional that he supposedly didn't hear, so he merely kissed her tenderly and told her he'd call.

When he got to his dad's hospital room, he was surprised to see Chaz there. His brother had flown back to California less than a week ago.

"Look who's here," his dad said, pointing to Chaz.

Will went over and shook his brother's hand. "Hey, when did you get in?"

"About an hour ago," Chaz said. He turned to their dad. "If you wanted me to stay longer for Thanksgiving, all you had to do was ask."

Their dad chuckled.

"How you feeling today, Dad?" Will asked.

"I'm fine," his dad said. "I told the doc I'm fine. I'm sick of being poked and prodded. These nurses won't even let me sleep at night. They just keep coming in the room, round the clock, to check my vitals."

"Yeah, they do that," Chaz said. "I remember. No fun."

Will's stomach churned as the guilt did another number on him. Chaz had been in the hospital for weeks after the accident.

They stayed for a little while, trying to cheer their dad up, before he finally kicked them out, saying he was tired.

"You want some coffee?" Chaz asked Will as they walked down the hospital hallway. "I'm wiped out from traveling."

"Sure. Let's go to the cafeteria so we can check in on him again."

"Yup."

They headed to the cafeteria and settled at a table with two large coffees. The cafeteria was depressing with its white walls and orange tables. The bright fluorescent lights were giving Will a headache. He rubbed his temples.

"You think he'll be okay?" Chaz asked.

Will nodded. "Yeah, Mom said the doctor said he should be fine now. He's too young to go."

Chaz drummed the table with his fingers. "Yeah, he's too stubborn to die. But he's got to stay on a really strict diet. You really think he'll follow it?"

"Mom will make him." He hesitated as his own worry swamped him. "Right?"

"Yeah, yeah. Right."

They both drank their coffee.

"You still mad about Carrie?" Chaz asked.

Will started. Carrie was the last thing on his mind. All he could think about was how close he came to losing his dad. Besides, Jasmine had stolen his heart and ran away with it. He couldn't imagine being with sweet, gentle Carrie now. She used to cry whenever they got into a fight. He was always walking on eggshells with her. He'd loved the way she took care of him and cooked for him, but he'd discovered he could do that stuff himself. Jasmine brought excitement to his life, not just physically. She was a match to him in all the best, crazy-making ways.

"Nah," Will said.

"Really?" Chaz asked.

"It's fine," he replied truthfully.

Chaz blew out a breath of relief. "Good. I can't tell you how guilty I felt about the whole thing. But the minute I laid eyes on her, it was like a freight train, ya know? Love at first sight."

Will didn't believe in love at first sight, but he let it go. When he'd first met Jasmine, sure he'd immediately noticed her beauty, her wild hair, but they'd rubbed each other entirely the wrong way. Of course, he'd been in a bad place in his life—stressed from taking over the orthodontic practice. Learning to manage a practice for the first time on his own with no help from his dad (who was on his retirement cruise) hadn't been easy. He'd been roped into the summer theater and mad at his dad for that too. Not to mention, still hurting over Chaz and Carrie. He was fine now. The practice was running smoothly, summer theater was over, and he was crazy about Jasmine. The only thing wrong in his life was sitting across the table from him.

Will cleared his throat. "Speaking of guilt…"

"Yeah?"

He stared at Chaz's cane propped up against the table. He shook his head. "Never mind."

"You feel guilty about the cane?"

Will's head jerked up, surprised. "Yeah," he admitted.

"It sucks," Chaz said.

Will's throat went tight. Of course it did. He knew that. "I'm sorry," he said, though it wasn't enough. It would never be enough.

"The accident sucked," Chaz said.

"It was all my fault," Will said. "You should've been the one to take over dad's practice."

Chaz held up a hand. "Whoa, whoa, whoa! Back it up. The accident sucked. This bum leg sucks. But I never would've been happy as an orthodontist. I was stuck in the first-born son expectations. That life never would've made me happy."

Will had never thought about it that way before. He'd always assumed Chaz wanted that life. "Really?"

Chaz nodded. "And now…" He grinned. "I'm so fucking happy I can't even believe it."

"Oh."

"The accident sucked, but good things came out of it. You don't have to feel guilty. Okay? I'm fine."

Will's eyes watered. He took a sip of coffee to cover up.

"Dad's going to be okay," Will said for his brother's sake.

"Yup." Chaz drank his coffee and looked away.

They sat in companionable silence, drinking their coffee, while Will tried to absorb the fact that Chaz had forgiven him. His head felt sort of strange, light-headed almost. He always felt especially bad when he saw Chaz, when he saw the evidence right in front of him of what he'd done.

Chaz pulled out his cell. "I'm going to check in with Carrie."

Will nodded absently as his brother headed outside to make the call. He thought about calling Jasmine, but he was still reeling from the fact that he'd been unexpectedly forgiven. He took a long walk instead. And when he returned, he felt lighter than he'd felt in years and years. Now if his dad would just be okay, and if Jasmine would just stop fighting him long enough to admit that she loved him as much as he loved her, his life would be perfect.

~ ~ ~

Jasmine answered the door that night surprised to see Will there, his hair rumpled like it got when he was stressed, his expression almost teary.

Her heart pounded. "What's wrong? Is it your dad?"

He stepped in and wrapped his arms around her. "No, he's fine. He's going to be okay."

She blinked back tears. "Oh, thank goodness."

He pulled back and held her hands. "Chaz forgave me."

She smiled. "See? What did he say?"

"He said he never would've been happy with the life he'd planned, so even though it sucked, it was also a good thing."

"I told you it would be good to talk to him."

He chucked her under the chin. "Don't get all full of yourself. I would've figured it out eventually."

"Mmm-hmm."

He searched her face. "Jaz, can I tell you something?"

She instantly felt wary. "What?"

"I love you."

Her throat closed with emotion. She could barely eke out one word. "Oh."

He released her hands and stepped back. "Oh? That's it?"

She shook her head, still all choked up. No guy had ever said those three words to her before and meant them.

"Admit it," he demanded. "You love me too."

Her hackles rose. "Will! You can't just demand someone love you."

"Dammit! I thought after last night—"

"Why do you keep pushing me to be a certain way? If you really loved me, you'd stop trying to change me."

"I'm not…" He shoved both hands in his hair, and it stayed all crazy the way she liked it best. "Forget it!"

"I do love you," she said softly. "I just got choked up."

He grabbed her and crushed her to him. After a few moments of a crushing hug, she pushed at his chest. "But you know as well as I do, we just bounce back and forth. Love and hate, love and hate."

"I never hated you," he said fiercely.

She untangled herself from his embrace because it was hard to think that way. "I mean the way we push each other's buttons. We fight so much. I don't want to fight anymore because now it hurts."

"Then we won't fight."

"You just got mad at me because I didn't say *I love you* back quickly enough."

"That's because I thought you were trying to deny it."

She blew out a breath. "It shouldn't be this hard. Love should be easy, at least in the beginning. I feel like we need therapy just to learn how to get along."

"We get along fine!" he barked.

"What are you so mad about?"

"You're trying to break up with me just because it's not easy!" He took a deep breath and lowered his voice. "Jaz. Come on. Please. Just…I'm sure it will get easier. We're still getting to know each other."

"I'm not breaking up with you. I'm just…worried. I think we can seriously damage each other at this point."

"We won't. We're good for each other."

She wasn't so sure. Now every fight felt painful. Every threat of separation felt terrifying. But looking into the future, thinking of how they might tear each other apart, also felt terrifying.

She looked at him—the man she couldn't live with, the man she couldn't live without.

He gazed back. Then he cupped her cheek. "I want to make love to you."

She took a step back. "See? That's another thing. You keep trying to push a certain way of sleeping with me when you know I don't like it."

"Jaz," he said gently. "You only cried because you felt something."

She frowned. "Very good, Dr. Levi. You win the shrink of the year."

He threw his hands in the air. "Have it your way. We'll just fuck. Happy?"

"No, I'm not happy! This is what I'm talking about! All these fights! All this trying to change me!"

"I'm not trying to change you! I'm trying to do what you wanted."

She shook her head. "That's not how you sounded.

You sounded smirky."

"I don't even know what the hell that means!" he hollered.

"Stop yelling at me!" she hollered back. "I don't want to fight."

"Me neither!"

She felt like crying. It was hopeless. They just couldn't stop going for each other's throats.

She pointed to the door. "I think you should go before one of us says something we'll regret."

"You drive me insane!" he hollered. "Freaking insane! You love me. You said it."

He wasn't getting out, and she couldn't take the fighting anymore, so she just grabbed her coat and purse, and left him there.

"This isn't over!" he yelled through the door.

She let out a breath and kept going. What was she supposed to do with him? This couldn't possibly be right. Her parents were so peaceful together. They never fought. This couldn't possibly be her future.

~ ~ ~

"Ladies, please, stop making this wedding blanket," Will said at knitting club two days later. It was painful to look at it. The blanket was nearly ready to piece together. "It's never going to happen. The love of my life belongs in an insane asylum."

"Come on, now," sweet Pam chided. "It can't be all that bad."

"Men always think it's the woman who belongs in the asylum," sour Diane said.

"Tell us what happened," crazy Maggie said, her eyes wide with gleeful anticipation.

He really didn't want to talk about their fight. It was so stupid. They loved each other, but that wasn't good enough for Jasmine. No, they had to be a picture-perfect couple before she'd even consider a future. Well, life wasn't perfect. Certainly his life had never been.

He went back to knitting and jolted in shock when Maggie snatched the needles right out of his hands. "Hey!"

"Speak!" Maggie demanded. "Or the scarf gets it." She put one hand on the edge of the row of stitches, ready to push it right off the needle. His heart clutched. She'd probably unravel the whole thing too. That scarf had taken him weeks. It was almost finished.

"She says we fight too much!" he exclaimed.

"Oh, that's okay." Maggie handed back the needles. He glowered and went back to knitting.

The room went quiet. Will looked up to find the women all staring at him.

"I think he needs an intervention," Maggie

declared.

"It's the only solution," Pam said.

The rest of the women were in agreement.

Will frowned. "I'm afraid to ask."

Maggie patted his arm. "Just leave everything to us."

Will was getting a bad feeling. "Don't do anything. Okay? You don't know her. She flies off the handle at the smallest thing. She's impossible."

"What do you think of the wedding blanket?" Maggie asked, showing him her section, which was the center, the most intricate part, a row of interlocking circles.

"It's gorgeous," he said. "How did you do the circles like that?"

Maggie exchanged a look with the other women that he couldn't quite interpret and explained to him how the cable stitch worked. "Why don't you give it a try?" she asked, handing him her needles and the cable needle.

He did. "It looks much more difficult than it really is."

She patted his arm. "Sure does, Will. It surely does."

~ ~ ~

Jasmine went to her parents' house for dinner on

Wednesday night, needing the comfort of home. Will must've been avoiding her because she never ran into him at work. He hadn't called or emailed, and neither had she. She felt like they were stuck, and she wasn't sure if they should try to move forward or back the hell up.

She let herself into her parents' house with her key and inhaled deeply the scent of pot roast. Her mom was such a good cook. Jasmine had been too busy with dance to spend much time in the kitchen with her. Not that she ever enjoyed food that much when she was competing so hard for her next job at all of those brutal auditions. She could never have an ounce of fat on her back then.

"Jasmine, is that you?" her mom called.

"It's me." She hung up her coat in the coat closet and headed back to the kitchen. "It smells heavenly. You want some help?"

"Why don't you make us a salad?" her mom suggested.

She got the fixings out of the fridge. "Where's Dad and Zoe?"

"Dad fell asleep in his chair again," her mom said with a shake of her head. "He stays up too late every night watching sports. Doesn't even have to be a live game. He'll watch reruns of games that happened years ago." She basted the pot roast. "Zoe's working tonight."

Jasmine threw the salad mix in the large salad bowl they always used. Then she went to rinse some carrots and cherry tomatoes. It was so peaceful at her parents' house. She let out a soft sigh. Home should be a haven. She tried to imagine sharing a home with Will—all fights and sex. Crazy. It would be crazy to let herself in for that kind of future.

"So how's Will's dad?" her mom asked.

"He's doing great. He'll have to watch his diet. He avoided surgery, so that's good." She'd visited Brian at home to see for herself and was glad to see he was back to his old wisecracking ways.

"Well, we all have to watch our diet now, don't we?"

"Yup." She dried off the carrots and peeled them. Little bits of carrot peel flew all over the sink. She'd pick it up later.

"And how's Will?" her mom asked carefully. Too carefully.

Jasmine turned. "Are people talking about us?"

"Well…" Her mom winced. "Nothing to be concerned about."

Damn busybodies in Clover Park. "What did you hear?"

Her mom waved that away. "I don't care about gossip. I care about my daughter. Is there anything you want to talk about?"

Jasmine rubbed her temple. "We just fight, Mom. Like all the time. It hurts. I don't know what to do. I don't want to fight anymore, but it's like we can't stop."

"Ah." Her mom poured herself a glass of water.

"That's it? No mother-daughter advice? Just *ah*."

Her mom tsked. "Sit down."

Jasmine sat next to her at the kitchen table.

"I hate to break it to you," her mom said, "but you got the worst of both worlds."

She scrunched her brows in confusion. "What are you talking about?"

"You've got your dad's temper and my sensitivity."

"What's so bad about that?" she demanded, hurt that her own mother pointed out her flaws.

Her mom shook her head. "It took a few years for your dad to learn how to argue with me so that I didn't end up in tears."

Her eyes went wide. She'd never heard her parents fight. "You and dad argue?"

Her mom smiled. "Sometimes. But we fight fair. No personal digs, just a difference of opinion. And, boy, does he have a lot of opinions!"

She snorted. That was certainly true.

"I think you and Will are very much alike," her mom said, taking her hand. "You wouldn't fight with him if he wasn't fighting right back. You're too aware of other people's feelings for that."

Jasmine felt like crying. They were doomed. "So, that's it? We're just never going to get along?"

"That's up to you and Will," her mom said gently. "What's more important to you? Letting your temper fly or getting along?"

"He does it too. It's not just me."

"Then that's a question you need to ask each other." Her mom patted her back. "I'm sure you'll work something out."

She looked at her mom with something close to desperation. "Or what?"

"Only you can answer that."

Her mom got out some rolls and butter, back to preparing dinner. Easy for her to be calm. Her life wasn't falling apart. She wasn't in love for the first time with the one man she couldn't get along with.

Jasmine went out the back door and let out a long scream of frustration. She returned to find her dad in the kitchen.

"What is wrong with you, girl?" he asked. "You woke me up. You woke the whole damn neighborhood up."

"It's your genes," she returned.

He turned to her mom in question. Her mom just shrugged. He turned back to Jasmine, took in her no-doubt rattled state. "Is Will giving you any trouble? Just say the word."

"Dad." Like she was really going to let her dad kick her boyfriend's ass.

"I'm not too old to win in a fight," he boasted, flexing his biceps.

"Ooh," her mom said, squeezing his bicep.

Jasmine rolled her eyes as her dad wrapped an arm around her mom's shoulders and pulled her close.

"Go see if we got any mail, Jaz," her dad said.

She gratefully headed out of the kitchen as she heard her mom say, "Hal," followed by a giggle and silence. Jasmine grabbed her coat and headed to the mailbox, not wanting to hear anymore of that lovey-dovey crap from the two people who gave her the worst of both worlds.

Chapter Thirteen

Will decided on Friday that the only way to get through to Jasmine was to wear her down. Besides, their wedding blanket was complete. Clearly, that was a sign that it was time for him to take the next step. He began his plan immediately and didn't let up for an entire week.

He accidentally on purpose ran into her in the shared hallway at work as much as possible. And when he did, he backed her up against the wall. It went the same way every time. He'd trap her against the wall, his hands on the wall on either side of her hips. Her breathing would quicken in anticipation.

"Will," she'd say in a soft shaky voice meant as a protest, only he knew her too well for that.

He ignored her shaky voice. Instead he cupped her cheek and slowly leaned down before pressing his mouth over hers as they fit together perfectly. He kissed her gently until she opened, and he swept his tongue inside, claiming her, tasting her. But still gently, tenderly, in the way that she very well knew meant he loved her with all his heart. And he knew his message got through because when he pulled away to gaze into her eyes, they were always shiny with tears. Her emotions, her tenderness back for him, overwhelmed her.

Then while she was still standing there, dazed from his kiss, he'd smile and walk away. She'd let out a string of curses in response.

And at the end of each workday, he'd stop by her studio and pick a fight with her. He wanted her to know he was part of her life now, whether they were kissing or fighting. What did they fight about? Her music. It was too loud. It really was. And she still hadn't soundproofed her side of the building. The hip-hop especially was grating. And when he'd had enough of her yelling at him, he'd start all over again—backing her up, trapping her, kissing her with all the love in his heart. She was weaker at night.

"Will, please," she'd say softly. He was definitely wearing her down.

"Kiss you again tomorrow," he'd return with a grin.

"Argh! This doesn't solve anything—"

He'd leave before she could start yelling.

He was pressing his point home—they belonged

together.

~ ~ ~

Jasmine threw herself into dance rehearsal over the next week for the Nutcracker recital her students were performing. Will seemed to make it his mission to keep her head spinning. He was either picking a fight with her or trying to overwhelm her with stolen tender kisses at her studio or in the hallway of their building. She refused to sleep with him under these circumstances—waffling between love and hate.

But then her world turned upside down, spun, and tilted on its axis, leaving her woozy.

It was the Saturday morning of the recital. She didn't have any classes because her students would be performing at the show that night. Still, she went to her studio and danced solo for the hell of it. Because that was who she was. She put on Tchaikovsky's *Nutcracker Suite* and did some ballet—arabesque, plié, pirouette. She did a whole series of chaînés tournes, quick turns diagonally across the dance floor. She leaped into a grand jeté as the music carried her along. She'd gotten four songs in when the door to the studio chimed.

She stepped out to answer it and found the women from Will's knitting club standing there. "Hi, everyone, come in. It's cold out there."

The older women, bundled up in parkas, knitted hats, and scarves, shuffled in to the waiting room.

"This is an intervention," Maggie announced.

"For Will," Pam put in.

"Oh," Jasmine said. "Did he, um, send you over here?" Will usually worked Saturday mornings. This was strange, even for him.

Shirley, Barbara, and Pat chorused at the same time. "He loves you."

"Love ain't perfect," Maggie said. Then she pulled a cream-colored hand-knit blanket out of a large bag. The women gathered around it, holding the edges so it spread out. It was large enough to fit on a queen-sized bed. Interlocking rings ran down the center.

Jasmine stared at it. "Wow! This is gorgeous." She took in all of the women, who were smiling proudly. "Did you make this yourselves?"

"Will helped," Pam said.

"That was one stitch," Diane protested.

"It still counts," Barbara caroled.

"It's for you," Maggie said. "It's your wedding blanket."

She staggered back, her heart pounding furiously. "My what? Where's Will?" She looked behind them. No Will.

"We have faith in you and Will," Pam said. "Do you?"

She bit her lip, and then she burst into tears. She covered her face with both hands. This was so embarrassing. She'd been crying way too much lately. She felt the blanket wrap around her, close and tight. She felt like she was being swaddled, and her entire body relaxed in the warmth.

"Whenever you fight," Maggie said. "Remember the love underneath it all."

"Let this blanket remind you that no matter how far apart you are," Pam said, "these interlocking rings will bind you together."

Jasmine sniffled and took them all in. "You guys play dirty."

"Damn right," Diane said.

The women grinned at each other. Then they unwrapped the blanket from her. She shivered from the loss of its warmth. Maggie folded it up and put it back in the bag. But then instead of handing it to her, Maggie turned to go.

"Wait!" Jasmine said. "Where are you going with my wedding blanket?"

"You'll get it back when you plan a wedding, girlie!" Maggie called. Then they were out the door.

Jasmine sank to a chair, completely overwhelmed as her mind reeled from the strange encounter.

~ ~ ~

That night at the recital, Jasmine was so proud of her students. They performed in the auditorium of Clover Park High. The three-year-olds played angels in cute little pink tutus with halos pinned to their hair. They managed to get through the ballet moves with her coaching them from the orchestra pit. One little girl yelled, "Hi, Daddy!" in the middle, but that was okay too. The audience, mostly parents, loved it. Even her adult tap class had put on a fantastic rendition of the toy soldiers' dance with Tony doing a hilarious bass drum to start them off. She'd taken liberties with the songs and styles of dance to accommodate her students. They had ballet, tap, jazz, modern dance, and hip-hop numbers in loose interpretations of the original production.

And then, after the applause, after the house lights went up, and people were leaving, Tony appeared at her side with roses.

"Great job tonight, teach," he said, handing her the roses.

"Aw, you didn't have to get me flowers," she said. "You guys did all the hard work. Good show."

"Thanks, but these aren't from me. They're from Will." He grinned and handed her a cell phone. She glanced down. It was Will's. Tony cued up a hip-hop playlist on the phone.

"What's going on?" she asked. This was so bizarre.

Will didn't even like hip-hop.

"Hit play after everyone leaves for an encore performance." Tony waggled his brows comically. "Dr. Foxy is waiting."

She stared at him in shock. Will hated that people called him Dr. Foxy. Tony chuckled and headed out the door. She sat in the front row, waiting. Curious, she ventured, "Will?"

"Did everyone leave?" he called from somewhere backstage.

"Almost."

"I'll wait."

Oh-kay. When everyone had left, she hit play.

Will bounded on stage wearing shades, a sideways Red Sox cap, a white tank top, basketball shorts, and red hi-top sneakers. He looked so bizarre, so different from the man she knew, but also irresistibly cute. A giant gold necklace with something dangling off the end hung around his neck. She leaned forward and squinted. Was that a gold molar?

He leaped into action, popping and locking, so it looked like he was standing then dropping a little, standing then dropping. Her jaw dropped. Where did he learn to do that? Had he been watching rehearsals? Then he threw to the floor, did a quick spin on his back, and tried to bounce back to his feet, but didn't quite make it. He scrambled off the floor and did some funky wave motions across his arms and then from his head to his toes. Then he did a glide, heading across the stage to the right, then back the other way.

He stopped abruptly, put his hands on his hips, and looked at her. "That's all I got."

She turned off the music and ran up the stairs to the stage. "What was that? Where did you get this outfit?" She picked up the necklace pendant. It *was* a molar. She giggled.

"Tony," he said. "The hat's mine."

She looked up to see his cheeks were pink. She grabbed him in a quick hug. "That was amazing." She pulled his shades off to find his eyes were serious. "But why did you do that?"

He gave her a slow smile. "That was me loosening up."

"Oh, Will." She stared into his eyes for a moment. Something was different. "Wait, where are your glasses?"

"I'm wearing contacts."

She smiled. He looked so cute without the glasses. "You should wear them more often."

"I see better with the glasses. I need them for work." He took her hands and looked into her eyes. "Listen, I know we keep trying to change each other, but here's the thing." He released one hand to cup her cheek. "The thing is, I don't think we need to change all that much. I think what we really just need is each other. You need my steady, straight-as-an-arrow ways. I need your looser, fun ways."

He meant she needed his tender ways, but he was too manly to ever admit that he was the more tender one in this relationship. Okay, fine, she was also tender, but he was more so. Rock steady was good, though. She hadn't had that since she'd left home. Her jobs had always been unpredictable in how long they'd last, the people in her life changed with the show, even her dance studio was filled with uncertainty as she tried to keep it afloat during its first year. And he sure as hell needed her much more fun side.

"Will, I love you and—" Her words were cut off by his kiss. She shoved his necklace out of the way and threw her arms around him as he kissed her slow and tender. She felt the love in his kiss down to her soul. No wonder she found him so hard to resist.

He broke the kiss, but kept his arms wrapped around her waist so she was still plastered against him. Then he smiled. Just kept smiling. Her hip-hop orthodontist.

"You were right," she said softly.

His brows shot up. "Speak up," he said with a grin. "I like where you're going with this."

She smiled. "You were right that I do have a tender side. I feel things deeply, more than anyone would ever guess, and…well, being in love for the first time—" She stopped to swipe at a tear that escaped. Will's gaze was full of understanding, so she barreled on. "Well, it was scary. It felt like my heart was out of my chest and sitting in your hands."

"I'll take good care of it," he promised. He tipped her chin up to look in her eyes. "It's so…I don't even know the word. It's so special that I'm your first love, but it's even more than that. It's…amazing. I'm so lucky."

"I don't want to fight anymore," she said. "It feels like you're stomping on my heart."

"But we're going to fight sometimes. Everyone does. And you have such a hot temper."

She pulled away. "I do not!"

He grinned. "So do I. We should have a safe word. When it gets too much, we say the word, and then we stop fighting until we can calm down."

"What word?"

He snagged her around the waist and pulled her back against him. His hand stroked down her back and cupped her bottom. "Make love?"

She gave him a look, but she still ran her hands up his warm, muscular arms. "That's two words."

"Fuck," he quickly amended.

She gave him a squinty-eyed look. "You really think I want to make love when we're fighting?"

"It would stop the fight. Yes?" His hand slid lower, cupping her sex.

"Will, be serious!"

"You are so hot for me right now."

She groaned, but still lifted her leg to wrap around his. "How about bow tie?" she teased.

He smiled down at her. "How about firecracker? Because that's what you are. You go off on me."

"I think it's the other way around." She rubbed herself against him, and he groaned before claiming her mouth. She ran her hands through his thick hair, and his sideways cap fell off. He didn't seem to notice. Then she slid her hands under his shirt, running up and down the planes of his warm back. She was just starting a foray toward the front when he broke the kiss.

"Agreed?" he asked, out of breath. "Firecracker?"

"Yes," she breathed. "Let's get out of here."

He started to go; then he stopped. "You almost made me forget with that sexy body of yours. Wait right here."

She smiled as he disappeared backstage and reemerged with a large gift bag. And in it was her wedding blanket. "It's back!" she exclaimed, hugging the blanket to her chest.

"Back?"

"I saw it this morning during the intervention.

You know, the ladies in your knitting club?"

He jammed his hands in his hair. "Intervention! I knew Maggie looked extra devious when I asked for the blanket. I told them not to do anything. What did they do?"

His hair was so wild and cute. "They told me these rings would bind us together and to remember the love underneath even when we're fighting." She blinked back tears.

He cupped her face with both hands. "I love you, Jasmine."

"I love you too," she said softly.

He went down on one knee. "Will you marry me?"

She burst into tears and got mad that she did, wiping her eyes furiously. "Yes." He wrapped his arms around her. "Wait!" She pulled the blanket from between them and wrapped it around both of them. He smiled and held her tight. "I hate when I cry," she said.

"I know you do." He kissed her hair. "Jaz, I heard you that night when you told me about Mark."

"Oh, God." She buried her head in his chest. "I'm so embarrassed."

"Don't be." His voice rumbled in his chest, and she met his eyes. "I'm glad you did. It made me realize how much I loved you. It made me want to marry you and spend the rest of my life making sure you felt safe and loved."

Another tear leaked out. He wiped it away with the pad of his thumb. "It's a good thing we found each other," he said. She nodded through her tears, until he added, "Or we'd just be a couple of dumb schmucks running around with our heads up our asses."

She laughed. "That's the most romantic thing anyone's ever said to me."

He smiled sheepishly. "I can do better." He kissed her gently. "You're my other half. You're my soul mate."

"That works," she managed over the lump in her throat.

He gave her a big smacking kiss on the lips and grinned. "I made an appointment to have my tattoo removed. To get rid of the reminder of my party days."

She wrapped her hands protectively around his bicep. "Don't you dare. This is my reminder that you have an inner stud."

"I do, huh?" He kissed her, and she returned it passionately. "I've got a new move for you," he whispered in her ear. "This one's all me."

She straightened. "Let's go, Dr. Levi."

He gestured in front of him. "After you, Jazzy."

She shook her finger at him. "Don't start that!" She carefully folded the blanket and put it back in the gift bag.

"Jazzy Levi." He put his Red Sox cap back on with a sideways swagger. "Has a nice ring to it."

"Firecracker," she said.

He held up one finger. "Amendment. Whoever says firecracker first, the other person has to give them a kiss."

"Firecracker, firecracker, firecracker."

He kissed her in the aggressive way she loved, so demanding as his tongue thrust in her mouth, as his hands pressed into her bottom, pressing her against his hardness, making her want to rip his shirt off before she remembered where they were.

She tore her mouth from his. "Will, please, I need—"

"I know what you need," he said in an arrogant way that made her smile. "Let's go home. You're moving in with me."

She tweaked his Red Sox cap. "You're so damn bossy."

"Firecracker," he said with a grin.

She kissed him again. They left, hand in hand, ready to rock each other's worlds, and fight, and make up, and love forevermore.

EPILOGUE

One year, nine months later…

Will could count on both hands everything that was going right in his life. He was a happily married man with a loving wife, a hot sex life, an awesome house, and a crazy-busy orthodontist practice thanks to a new kickass website and monthly bowling parties organized by Tony and Hillary for their patients. Tony and Hillary were a couple now. Will had warned Tony about the perils of a workplace romance, but Jasmine had told him to butt out. Tony and Hillary seemed pretty happy. Will also had his health, a sweet orange tabby cat, an adorable nephew, and a new dance hobby. He knew all sorts of dances now and loved dancing with Jasmine at home. He could go on and on about all the things that were right in his life, but the best thing was happening right now.

"You'll pay for this, Will!" Jasmine screamed as another contraction hit.

"Honey, you're crushing my fingers," he said gently.

Will glanced at Pam, the certified nurse midwife who was with them at the birthing center. She nonchalantly turned away, giving them some privacy. Pam and Diane from knitting club turned out to be certified nurse midwives who worked at a birthing center in nearby New York. Jasmine had wanted a home birth. The birthing center adjacent to the hospital was their compromise. Jasmine loved the whirlpool and walking around the grounds, but once the contractions hit in earnest she'd returned to the bed, lying on her side, alternating angry and weepy.

He leaned close to whisper in his wife's ear. "Shh, Jaz, you're doing great."

Jasmine panted as the pain passed. "And you're so tender and loving," she said softly. "I'm sending your mom flowers for raising you right."

He stroked her hair. "You don't have to do that."

She got all weepy again. "And your dad should get something for bringing us together."

"How about me?" he asked. "What do I get?"

She smiled. "You get me."

He smiled back and handed her some ice chips to suck on. "Pretty soon little Sammie will be here."

"You mean Ella," she said around the ice chips.

"I'm sure I planted a boy in there." He was

actually hoping for a girl too, but kept the argument going because it seemed to make her happy to argue regularly. As long as it wasn't mean-spirited. It was sort of a hobby of theirs. The good part started with a "firecracker" and ended with a bang.

Another contraction hit. "You tricked me, Will Levi! With your soft words and tender loving!"

Will's cheeks and ears burned. Did she have to use his full name? There were birthing rooms on either side of theirs. Pam chuckled and came over to check on his wife.

Jasmine turned to Pam. "I wanted power sex, but no-oo-oo! Will had to make love! This is what happens!"

Pam nodded sympathetically. After the contraction passed, Pam checked her dilation. "Almost there, Jasmine. You're doing great."

Pam sat in a chair in the corner to wait. Jasmine calmed down. He took that opportunity to assure her of future lovemaking.

"As soon as the doc clears you," he whispered, "I promise to power sex you so hard."

"Oh, Will." Her eyes got shiny with tears. "You're so good to me."

He stroked her cheek. "I love you. And admit it, you like the tender loving."

"I love you too." She got weepy. "I do like the

tender loving, but I miss the other kind. It's been nine months."

"We'll get there," he soothed.

"You never fight with me anymore," she pouted. "How do I know you really love—aahh! This is all your fault!"

The contractions were definitely getting closer together now.

"Will Levi!" she bellowed. "You're going down!"

Will rubbed her arm in sympathy.

One hour later, Jasmine was getting tired and burst into tears. "I can't do it, Will! I can't! It's too hard."

He took her hand. "Hey, you're strong. You can do this." Not like she had a choice at this point. The baby was almost here.

She looked away. "No, I can't."

He tipped her face toward him so he could look in her eyes. "You are my warrior goddess," he said fiercely. "Now I want you to dig deep. No more screaming. Focus all your energy inward. Ride that wave." That's what they'd taught them in birthing class. To ride the wave of the contraction.

She glared at him. "That wave idea was stupid. This is more like a freaking choke hold on my uterus."

He went on. "And you push our boy out with a warrior's battle cry."

She got quiet. That was good. She was focusing inward. Hopefully she'd stop screaming at him now. He watched as Jasmine amazed him. She rode the waves of the contractions that came harder and closer together, quietly, focused on her breathing, until she announced, "I want to push."

Twenty minutes later, Jasmine let out a warrior's battle cry as Ella arrived with a cry to rival her mother's. Will took one look at his daughter and fell in love. He watched as Pam checked over the baby, swaddled her in a blanket, and handed her to Jasmine. Will quietly wiped away tears as Jasmine cuddled their daughter close.

"I was right," Jasmine said, smiling at him. "It's a girl."

He stroked Ella's cheek. "I'm so happy."

"Me too."

He kissed his wife tenderly, until Ella bellowed for attention. "She's a spitfire like her mom."

"She'll dance," Jasmine said, putting the babe to her breast.

He gazed at Ella with her tiny little fingers. "Maybe she'll be an orthodontist."

"A grand tradition," Jasmine said with a grin.

As it turned out, Ella did neither. She became a filmmaker—writing, directing, and acting in her own films. And the first story she wrote and acted out, in third grade no less, was that of her crazy parents who loved to fight and dance and kiss. Just like every good love story in every animated movie she'd ever seen. Her teacher, Mrs. O'Hare, loved it. Everyone loved it when she performed it at the Clover Park Elementary Talent Show too, though her two younger brothers thought it was gross and mushy. Ella became known for movies featuring strong heroines on grand adventures and the tender heroes that loved them.

-THE END-

Thanks for reading *Almost Over It*. I hope you enjoyed it! The other books in The Clover Park STUDS Series, *Almost in Love* and *Almost Married* are out now!

See how it all began when crazy Maggie's (from knitting club) great-grandbabies were just a gleam in her eye in *The Opposite of Wild*. Turn the page to read an excerpt from *The Opposite of Wild*, Ryan and Liz's story.

THE OPPOSITE OF WILD

KYLIE GILMORE

Unleash the wild woman…?

Ex-cop Ryan O'Hare takes one look at buttoned-up control freak Liz Garner and just itches to loosen the woman up. Not that he's into her. Because a woman like that comes with way too many expectations. Not to mention, she practically works for him, and he didn't hire Liz to watch after his beloved Harley-stealing Gran so he could turn Liz loose in his bed. Still, there's something about her, a hidden wild side, that makes him wonder what it would take.

Liz must be crazy to work for the insensitive, arrogant, horribly…hot man she's avoided for years. Unfortunately, she needs the money and Ryan's grandmother needs a keeper. (Midnight tango lessons and ziplines with Gran, anyone?) Ryan's rare smile and swaggering confidence have Liz torn between throwing her favorite pinot grigio at his head or throwing herself at him. Can this control freak find a way to let loose with the tough, no-strings guy who once broke her heart?

CHAPTER ONE

Ryan O'Hare sat at the swank bar of the Four Seasons Hotel New York, the beer in front of him untouched, as he kept an eye on his mark. The short, bald man in a suit at the other end of the bar hadn't ordered yet, and his eyes nervously scanned the lobby. Ryan's phone vibrated. He glanced at the number, his younger brother Travis. *Not now. I'm waiting for the money shot.*

A young redhead—twenty-five at the most—in a skintight blue dress that barely covered her ass approached, working those hips. He slid the microcamera from his pocket and waited. *Quick kiss hello on the lips. That's a start.* Now he just needed proof they went someplace private together. He'd have to wait for however many drinks it took the soon-to-be divorced Stew Harbinger to get this one up to his room. Stew's hand slid up her inner thigh—not too long a wait.

His cell vibrated again. Another message from Trav. Dammit. Trav knew he was working tonight. He ignored it. Mrs. Harbinger wanted before and after pictures of her cheating husband for the divorce battle to come. Cheating spouses were the bulk of his private investigator business.

Marriage was a crock.

Stew pulled a velvet box from his pocket. The redhead was delighted. Diamond earrings. *Oh, Stewie. You're going to pay for those.* He snapped a few more pictures. His cell vibrated. This time a text from Trav: *Call me. It's about Gran.*

Ryan tensed. Gran was seventy-two and had walked away from a car accident last week on Route 84 without a scratch on her. A fucking miracle. She'd been sideswiped by a truck in her little Corolla, did a few three-sixties across two lanes of traffic and landed on the grassy median. The ER doctor had said she was fine. Still, he and his brothers had taken turns checking in on her over the past week. He'd even placed an ad for more regular care this summer. She'd been doing odd things since the accident, like eating Snickers for breakfast and skipping her cholesterol pills. His sweet gran had even called him an old nag just for checking in on her.

He took one last look at Stew and the redhead cooing at each other, decided to risk it, and slipped out to the marbled lobby to call Trav back. "It's Ryan. What's up?"

"Now don't go ballistic…"

Ryan said nothing. Trav always spilled his guts to fill the silence.

True to form, Trav spilled. "I just saw Gran, and she was really happy."

"Yeah, so? That's good." He scanned the lobby in case Stew and his lover headed for their hotel room.

"When I asked her why, she said it was because she took your Harley out for a ride and, I quote," Trav's voice rose to a falsetto, "'felt the wind in my hair.'"

Ryan let out a string of curses that had heads turning. He lowered his voice. "Who gave her the keys?"

"She said she wanted to leave you a lasagna. I gave her my key to your place."

How the hell did she know his Harley keys were in his kitchen drawer? Gran on a Harley. She was seventy-two freaking years old! He paced back and forth, imagining all the worst-case scenarios—her frail body flattened or crumpled on the side of the highway. Nothing could happen to her. He wouldn't let it.

"You still there, buddy?" Trav asked.

He jammed a hand through his hair. "I'm changing the locks on the garage. And don't give her my key ever again!"

"Sorry, Ry. But Gran and the Harley are both fine. I just thought you should know. Maybe you could talk some sense into her."

Ryan rubbed his throbbing temple at the headache already building there. "I'll talk to her." His grandmother needed a keeper ASAP. He pocketed his phone and slipped back into the bar.

Dammit! Stew and the redhead were gone.

~ ~ ~

Liz Garner grabbed her cell phone off the kitchen counter, whirled, and aimed the tiny camera at the code on the tub of hummus. "Fitness Woman," she sang as the nutrition label popped up on the screen and saved to her MyFoodBuddy app. Fifty calories per serving.

She wished she wasn't celebrating the last day of school alone tonight, but the other teachers were all married with kids. She arranged the chopped veggies by color in a large bowl around the hummus and reminded herself there was nothing wrong with being single. Thirty was the new twenty-five, right? So what was a two-year dry spell? She snatched the pinot grigio from the fridge. It wasn't like she'd shrivel up and die from lack of—

The doorbell rang, startling her. She wasn't expecting any visitors.

She peeked through the peephole and flung open the door. "Daisy! You should've called me. I'd have picked you up at the train station."

Her older sister stood on the other side of the door, her long, blond hair up in a messy ponytail, her eyes red and puffy. "I took a cab. Oh, Liz," she cried before throwing her arms around her sister.

Liz blinked and pulled back to look at what pressed between them. Through the outline of Daisy's flowing pink sundress was an unmistakable baby bump.

She gasped. "Daisy, you're—"

"I know!" she exclaimed before bursting into tears.

Omigod. Liz guided her to the sofa. Daisy had to be at least six months along, and not once had she given a clue about her current predicament—single, pregnant, and living on a receptionist's salary. Handing her a tissue, she put a comforting arm around Daisy's heaving shoulders. Daisy leaned in and sobbed into Liz's favorite lavender button-down shirt. *Daisy is my priority. I'll have the shirt dry-cleaned tomorrow.*

She waited until Daisy's sobs slowed before gently urging, "Tell me everything."

"Can I get a drink of water?" Daisy asked in a shaky voice.

"Of course." She got a glass out of the cabinet and poured filtered water from the pitcher.

My impulsive, flighty sister—a mother? Children need structure, routine.

Liz would take care of everything. Even though she was the younger sister by three years, she'd been looking out for Daisy for as long as she could remember. Covering for her, making excuses for her, and when Liz was old enough, helping Daisy fix whatever mess she'd made, of which there'd been plenty. From sneaking out on school nights to meet her friends, to underage parties in the woods, to joy rides without a license. Their parents still didn't know about most of that stuff. The driving without a license they did know. Daisy was a speed demon and got pulled over her first time out. And her fifth time. A few more times after that too.

Liz peered over the half wall separating the kitchen and living room. "Are you hungry?"

"Always," Daisy replied, reaching into her bright orange and purple boho bag and pulling out a box of Sno-Caps.

A flash of alarm went through Liz. She snagged the veggies and hummus bowl, grabbed the water, and hurried back to the living room.

"Why don't we save this for later?" she asked, neatly substituting the veggie bowl for the Sno-Caps in Daisy's hand. She slipped the candy behind a cushion to be disposed of later.

Daisy merely shrugged and dug into the veggies. "You wouldn't believe how hungry being pregnant can make you."

"Why didn't you tell me?" Liz asked softly. Daisy had always called her at the first sign of trouble. It stung that it had taken her this long.

Daisy set the veggie bowl on the coffee table and sighed. "At first, I was just in shock. Did you know the pill isn't one hundred percent when you're on antibiotics?"

Liz shook her head.

"Well, it's not. Then I thought, *I can't keep this baby*. I don't know the first thing about babies. I'm not married. I have no money. I share an apartment with two roommates." She gripped her hands tightly together. "I even went to the clinic, but I couldn't go through with it."

"I'm glad," Liz managed. She'd almost lost her niece or nephew. It hurt to think about. Her own biological clock had been ticking louder and louder.

"I'm still not ready," Daisy confessed. "I wake up in the middle of the night in a cold sweat that I forgot the baby somewhere, or I don't have enough money to feed it, or that it rolls off one of those tiny little changing stations they have in the ladies' room." Her voice came out tiny and choked at the end. She took a deep breath. "I'm giving the baby up for adoption."

"No!" Liz stood in her agitation. "We'll back out of the contract. Mothers have rights. Wait, did you sign anything?"

"Not yet—"

"Well, *don't*. We'll raise the baby together." Her mind flew. "We can take childcare in shifts! I'll take afternoon to night, so you can waitress at Garner's, and you take the school day—"

"I'm getting too big to be on my feet—"

"We'll put you at the hostess stand. Mom and Dad will get you on Garner's insurance plan. And you can live here. You can have my room and—"

"Oh, I couldn't take your bed," Daisy protested.

"You wouldn't be comfortable on the sofa. Anyway, it's just until you're ready for a place of your own." *Or a bigger place for the three of us.*

Daisy's blue eyes, so like her own, reflected equal parts hope and worry. "Are you sure?"

She sat next to Daisy and took her sister's hands in hers. "I'm sure. And you wouldn't have come to me tonight if you hadn't been having doubts about the adoption. We'll get through this together. You are *not* alone."

"I know," Daisy said with a watery smile. "Sorry." She choked out a laugh. "Damn hormones make me cry at insurance commercials. You know the one where the squirrel almost gets hit by that car?"

Liz nodded solemnly.

Daisy rubbed a hand over her belly. "It's a boy. Seven months already." She fumbled around in her bag and pulled out an ultrasound picture.

Liz clapped a hand over her mouth and blinked back tears. *Omigod, I'm going to be an aunt!* He was so beautiful. She could see his face with pursed lips, a tiny button nose, closed eyes. His body was curled up, with one hand on the side of his head. "Oh, Daisy! When are you due?"

"August twenty-second. I haven't told Mom and Dad yet, so don't say anything."

Liz kept quiet. The people of Clover Park, Connecticut, were not known for their discretion. Their parents were sure to hear the happy news the moment Daisy stepped foot out of this apartment. She glanced at her sister chomping on a red pepper slice and tossing back the box of Sno-Caps. So much for her hiding place. "Um…does the father want to be involved?" *And do you know who the father is?*

Daisy shook her head. "He's a minor league baseball player on the Norwalk Tigers. He didn't want anything to do with the baby." She looked away.

"He should still pay child support," Liz said, instantly angry at this stupid ball player.

"It's fine. We were only together that one time."

Liz's lips formed a tight line. She didn't plan on

letting the father get off that easy, but she let it go for now.

"I might need to borrow some money too." Daisy grimaced, but plowed on. "I don't have much in savings, kinda just live paycheck to paycheck, but a baby needs things."

Liz was almost afraid to ask. "How much?"

"Ten thousand dollars?"

Her head throbbed. "Ten thousand? I don't have ten thousand dollars! Does it really cost that much to have a baby?"

Daisy looked down at her hands. "I have some credit card debt. The interest alone is eating up my paycheck."

Not that a temp job at a spa in New York City was ever going to be much of a paycheck. Liz wished, not for the first time, that Daisy would stick with something and work her way up to a better paying position. Daisy was smart, but she'd dropped out of college her first year and had a series of odd jobs ever since. Maybe Liz could get her into community college. *One thing at a time*, Liz reminded herself.

Daisy continued. "I paid the minimum each month, and it just got worse and worse. Going out with my friends, traveling, clothes, shoes, purses, makeup. But that's all done, I swear!" She lifted a hand in promise. "I transferred all my debt to a lower interest credit card, but still…it's bad. Liz, I promise I'll do everything I can think of to pay down this debt, and I won't ever ask you for another cent again. Things are different for me now with the baby, and I want a chance to turn over a new leaf for both of us."

Looking from her sister's earnest expression to her pregnant belly, a lump formed in Liz's throat. She'd help out; of course she would. Nothing was more important to Liz than family. Their sisterly bond was tight. She'd do anything for Daisy, and Daisy would do the same. Daisy had come through when Liz's fiancé Craig dumped her two weeks before the wedding, taking care of cancelling the wedding plans and notifying all the guests. Her sister might flutter to wherever the wind blew her, but she always came through for Liz when it really counted, and she never broke a promise.

"I'll find a summer job," Liz said, "but you have to swear everything I give you goes toward paying down that debt and for the baby. No shopping sprees."

"I swear it will!" Daisy's eyes filled with tears. "Thank you so much! You are the best sister and aunt ever!" She stood, arms open, and when Liz stood to hug her, Daisy threw herself into her arms, hiccupping, crying, and laughing all at once.

Liz held her tighter, her own eyes stinging with unshed tears. Liz would have the baby she longed for, even if it wasn't her white picket fence dream-husband, kids (one boy, one girl), nonshedding dog. She'd be the best aunt this child could ever want.

After they watched the movie Liz had planned for tonight, *Bringing Up Baby*-how appropriate, though Baby was a leopard-Liz settled on the sofa. She'd be lying if a tiny part of her wasn't jealous. She'd been so close to her white picket fence dream two years ago. Right up until Craig dumped her for his pregnant-by him-secretary. She'd done everything right, yet here she was single and childless while Daisy had led the life of the wild woman. And now she had what Liz always wanted most.

She sighed. None of that stuff mattered now. The important thing was her nephew. She already loved him so much.

She grabbed her laptop. She had two students lined up for tutoring, but it wasn't enough money. She didn't want to work for her parents at Garner's Sports Bar & Grill. Too many of her students and their families went there. It would be tough to keep authority in the classroom if she waited on the kids during the summer. Settling on the sofa again, she wrapped her fleece blanket around her shoulders and opened her laptop. First, she pulled up QuickBooks and added the expense of the wine she still hadn't tasted. She liked to keep a daily accounting of expenses to make sure she stayed in her budget. Her account balance was enough to get through the summer, but not nearly enough to make a dent in Daisy's debt.

She searched job websites for summer help. They were hiring at the mall over in Eastman, only minimum wage, and she'd likely be working with a lot of teenagers, feeling ancient. After a wasted half hour of searching, she remembered *The Clover Park Record* had job listings in the back.

She carefully pulled the newspaper off her neat pile of to-be-read items. Luckily she hadn't read it yet or it would already be recycled. Running her finger down the classifieds, she found exactly three job listings: the paper needed volunteer reporters to cover town meetings, a local moving company needed summer help (at five foot four and no muscle, she was way underqualified for that one), and someone was looking for an elder care provider. Now *that* she could do.

She'd call first thing in the morning. She set the paper back on the end table, curled up on the sofa, and was asleep within minutes. She woke the next day to the sound of her sister shuffling around in the kitchen, banging cabinet doors, probably looking for the cereal.

"Mornin'," Liz said when she entered the kitchen.

"Mornin'," Daisy muttered. She never had been much of a morning person.

"Go ahead and sit," Liz said. She got out the

Cheerios, milk, bowl, and spoon and set it in front of Daisy. Then she poured her a small glass of orange juice.

"Thank you," Daisy said. "No one has taken care of me in so long." Her eyes teared up.

Geez, pregnancy hormones do make you cry at everything.

"Just this one time, then you find your own breakfast," Liz said briskly, trying to detour another crying jag. It was too early for all the drama, and she had a phone call to make.

Daisy nodded and dug into her cereal. Liz grabbed her cell and took it into her bedroom for privacy. She dialed, and after a few rings, it went to voice mail.

"You've reached Ryan O'Hare. Leave a message."

She dropped the phone.

Her heart galloped at an alarming speed. *Ryan O'Hare.* The man she'd spent years avoiding, ever since The Humiliation. Ryan O'Hare was hiring an elder care provider? She grabbed her cell off the floor and jabbed the end button to hang up.

She paced her bedroom and tried to think. *Should I call back? How badly do I need this job?*

She took a deep breath and dialed again, clenching her teeth as she heard his voice on the recorded message. Then, all in a rush, she left a message. "Hello, this is Liz Garner. I'm calling about the ad you placed for an elder care provider. I live in town and have many references, so please call me to arrange an interview." She left her number and hung up.

Then she collapsed on her bed and screamed into a pillow.

Get The Opposite of Wild now!

Also by Kylie Gilmore

The Clover Park Series

THE OPPOSITE OF WILD (Book 1)
DAISY DOES IT ALL (Book 2)
BAD TASTE IN MEN (Book 3)
KISSING SANTA (Book 4)
RESTLESS HARMONY (Book 5)
NOT MY ROMEO (Book 6)
REV ME UP (Book 7)

The Clover Park STUDS Series

ALMOST IN LOVE (Book 1)
ALMOST MARRIED (Book 2)
ALMOST OVER IT (Book 3)

Acknowledgments

Thanks to my boys, who've required several orthodontic appointments, which made me wonder if an orthodontist could ever be a sexy hero. Will can, for sure! Thanks to my hubby, the sexy hero in my life, who makes sure my men sound like real men. Thanks, as always, to Tessa, Pauline, Mimi, Shannon, Kim, Maura, and Jenn for all you do. And thank you dear reader for going on this wild ride with me!

About the Author

Kylie Gilmore is the *USA Today* bestselling romance author of the Clover Park series and the Clover Park STUDS series. She writes quirky, tender romance with a solid dose of humor.

Kylie lives in New York with her family, two cats, and a nutso dog. When she's not writing, wrangling kids, or dutifully taking notes at writing conferences, you can find her flexing her muscles all the way to the high cabinet for her secret chocolate stash.

Praise for Kylie Gilmore

THE OPPOSITE OF WILD

"This book is everything a reader hopes for. Funny. Hot. Sweet."
—New York Times Bestselling Author, Mimi Jean Pamfiloff

"Ms. Gilmore's writing style draws the reader in and does not let go until the very end of the story and leaves you wanting more."
—Romance Bookworm

"Every aspect of this novel touched me and left me unable to put it down. I pulled an all-nighter, staying up until after 3 am to get to the last page."
—Luv Books Galore

DAISY DOES IT ALL

"The characters in this book are downright hilarious sometimes. I mean, when you start a book off with a fake life and immediately follow it by a rejected proposal, you know that you are in for a fun ride."
—The Little Black Book Blog

"Daisy Does It All is a sweet book with a hint of sizzle. The characters are all very real and I found myself laughing along with them and also having my heart ripped in two for them."
—A is for Alpha, B is for Book

BAD TASTE IN MEN

"I gotta dig a friends to lovers story, and Ms. Gilmore's 3rd book in the Clover Park Series hits the spot. A great dash of humor, a few pinches of steam, and a whole lotta love...Gilmore has won me over with everything I've read and she's on my auto buy list...she's on my top list of new authors for 2014."
—Storm Goddess Book Reviews

"The chemistry between the two characters is so real and so intense, it will have you turning the pages into the midnight hour. Throw in a bit of comedy – a dancing cow, a sprained ankle, and a bit of jealousy and Gilmore has a recipe for great success."
—Underneath the Covers blog

KISSING SANTA

"I love that Samantha and Rico are set up by none other than their mothers. And the journey they go on is really hilarious!! I laughed out loud so many times, my kids asked me what was wrong with me."
—Amazeballs Book Addicts

"I absolutely adored this read. It was quick, funny, sexy and got me in the Christmas spirit. Samantha and Rico are a great couple that keep one another all riled up in more ways than one, and their sexual tension is super hot."
—Read, Tweet, Repeat

Thanks!

Thanks for reading *Almost Over It*. I hope you enjoyed it. Would you like to know about new releases? You can sign up for my new release email list at Eepurl.com/KLQSX. I promise not to clog your inbox! Only new release info and some fun giveaways. You can also sign up by scanning this QR code:

I love to hear from readers! You can find me at:
kyliegilmore.com
Facebook.com/KylieGilmoreToo
Twitter @KylieGilmoreToo

If you liked Will and Jasmine's story, please leave a review on your favorite retailer's website or Goodreads. Thank you!

22605536R00158